HEARTSTRINGS

Barbara Wilson

BANTAM BOOKS
NEW YORK • TORONTO • LONDON • SYDNEY • AUCKLAND

HEARTSTRINGS
A BANTAM BOOK : 0 553 56484 6

First publication in Great Britain

PRINTING HISTORY
Bantam edition published 1996

Cover photo by Paula Retsky

Bantam Books are published by Transworld Publishers Ltd,
61–63 Uxbridge Road, Ealing, London W5 5SA,
in Australia by Transworld Publishers (Australia) Pty Ltd,
15–25 Helles Avenue, Moorebank, NSW 2170,
and in New Zealand by Transworld Publishers (NZ) Ltd,
3 William Pickering Drive, Albany, Auckland.

Printed and bound in Great Britain by
Cox & Wyman Ltd, Reading, Berkshire.

Chapter One

I remember thinking it was a close to perfect day. Everything seemed to be going right. Or at least it was until I found out that my parents had decided to totally ruin my life.

I can hear Mom now. "Aren't you being a bit melodramatic, Tess?" This from a woman who writes romance novels just dripping with melodrama. I mean, if I tend to overdramatize things, and I guess I do, it must be genetic.

But to get back to that nearly perfect day. It was the middle of May, with crab apple trees blooming clouds of pink and white all over town. School at Glen Forest High was in the final wrap-up and everyone was in a festive countdown-to-summer mood. My friends and I were already planning our usual summer outings—swimming in Lake Michigan, shopping in the city, going to all the blockbuster summer movies and rock concerts. It promised to be fun, fun, fun.

My classes were all winding up just great too. I had gotten an A+ on my history paper, and Ms. Porter, my English teacher, told me she was submitting one of my short stories to a statewide fiction contest. Naturally, I was thrilled.

But the real highlight of the day came during chorus. Music has always been the real focus of my life. Mom and Dad were always eager to encourage my musical ambitions. They had me take voice and piano lessons, and then guitar when I turned eleven and decided I wanted to be a rock star.

Of course, high school chorus is a far cry from Madonna, but it's always been my favorite thing at school. That day when I got to chorus a bunch of kids were mobbed around the bulletin board. My friend Melissa ran over to me, all excited.

"Tess, you've made Note-ables!"

I was so happy I could have burst into song like they do in those old cornball movies. Note-ables is a select group chosen from the chorus to perform at special events. Since only the best singers get picked, it's a great honor. I was going to have the most fabulous junior year that anyone could ever have!

Just when I thought things couldn't possibly get any better, Michael Wright appeared and said, "Hey, Tess, you're in. Welcome to the club." He smiled at me and I felt my knees grow weak.

I managed to say, "Thanks, Michael." I should explain that Michael Wright was the most adorable, wonderful male in the entire school, and did he ever have a terrific voice! Now that I was in Note-ables, Michael would get to know me. It wasn't totally inconceivable that he would fall madly in love with me.

This wonderful fantasy entertained me for the rest of the day and all the way home. As my school bus travelled the familiar suburban streets, I decided that God was truly in his heaven and all was right with the world. All I needed to make my life perfect was my own car, and I was sure I'd soon be able to wheedle my parents into getting me one. After all, I'd had my driver's license for almost a month now.

When I reached my house, I was surprised to see Dad's car in our driveway. That was pretty unusual, because I don't think Dad had ever gotten home before seven o'clock. Dad is a real overachieving yuppie. He made vice president of Cookie Crumbles, Inc. when he was only thirty-seven. You're probably familiar with the Cookie Crumbles company. Although it's fairly new, it's really been giving those Keebler elves a run for their money over the past few years. I may be prejudiced, but I think my dad had a lot to do with that.

As I walked up our driveway, I wondered what he was doing home so early. I had a sudden sense of panic that only some crisis could have dragged him away from the office so early. I started imagining all sorts of terrible things as I dashed to the back sunporch, where the door was usually open. I stopped in my tracks when I saw Mom and Dad sitting there. Dad was sprawled in a lounge chair, a glass of wine in his hand and a huge smile on his face. A wave of relief flooded me, and I continued on into the porch.

"And here's Tess," Dad said as if he was

4

overjoyed to see me, "home from a hard day at school."

I tossed my books on a table, sat down, and grinned. "Yeah, it was rough all right. But what's with you, Dad? What are you doing home? You didn't get fired or anything, did you?"

I was just joking, but Mom and Dad quickly exchanged a look, and it made me suddenly nervous. Turning from one to the other, I said, "C'mon, what's up, you guys?"

Mom smiled at me. "Your dad has some good news, Tess."

"Yeah, Tess," said Dad a trifle too heartily. "Really good news. But—well, it's sort of good news and bad news."

Sometimes your parents can drive you absolutely crazy! I shook my head. "Well, what's the *good* news?"

Dad took a sip of his wine and said, "Cookie Crumbles is opening a new plant down south and I'm going to be head of it."

Did you ever have the wind knocked out of you? That's how I felt.

"I know it's something of a shock . . ." Dad went on.

"Something of a shock?" I echoed. "You're

5

going to be in charge of a new plant down south? What do you mean by south? Tinley Park?"

Dad managed not to laugh. "Sorry, honey. I'm not talking about the south suburbs. I'm talking about the south, as in Kentucky."

"Kentucky?" I repeated, disbelieving. "You mean we're going to have to *move*?"

"I'm afraid so, Tess. I hate to pull you away from your friends and school . . ."

"Then why are you?" I wailed.

"I'm sorry, kiddo," Dad said, "but I don't have any choice. This great deal just fell in our laps. A new factory down in Kentucky was just put up for sale and it was perfect for our operation. We'll be able to start up by the fall."

The fall! Everything was suddenly hopeless. My wonderful day that had held so much promise for the future had suddenly evaporated, *poof*, right into thin air.

"When did you plan to move?" I asked glumly, feeling like a convict waiting to find out her execution date.

"Well, we'll put the house up for sale right away," Dad said.

I felt sick. He was talking about getting rid of the only home I had ever known!

Mom came over and put a hand on my

shoulder. "I know it'll be hard leaving here. I love this house too, Tess."

I couldn't look at her because I knew if I did I would burst into tears. "So where is this place, anyway?" I muttered sullenly.

"It's a small town called Blossom Creek," Dad told me.

"Blossom Creek?" I echoed incredulously. "It sounds like some podunk town full of hicks, and I suppose I'll be going to Hicksville High!"

Dad was starting to get annoyed at me. "Get off your high horse, kiddo," he said. "It's a nice little town and the people there are really friendly. I know it'll be different from what you're used to, but it's only an hour from Louisville. We'll still have a city nearby."

Mom joined in the Blossom Creek booster club. "Your dad thought we could buy some acres in the country, Tess."

"How can you guys do this to me?" I shouted, my shock suddenly giving way to anger. "How can you drag me away from my school, my friends, from—from *everything*!"

"Honey, I know you're upset, but really, it won't be so bad," Mom said. It was sort of like when the nurse tells you it won't hurt a bit and then stabs you with a huge needle.

"Not so bad?" I yelled. "I was going to have probably the most terrific year ever, and now you're forcing me to move to some awful place in Kentucky! My whole life is just wrecked!"

I raced out of the porch, making a beeline for the stairs. I knew Mom and Dad would leave me alone for a while. They were probably feeling guilty. *Good!* I thought. *I hope they feel guilty as anything!* But what did that matter? It wouldn't change a thing. We were moving to Blossom Creek, Kentucky, and there was nothing I could do to stop it.

I rushed into my room, flung myself on my bed, and cried.

My final two weeks at Glen Forest High rolled by. Instead of being overjoyed at the prospect of summer stretched out in front of me, I was utterly depressed. Of course, my friends tried to buck me up. They were appalled to hear that I was moving. They promised to write and call, and urged me to come back and visit them as soon as possible. That cheered me up for maybe five minutes.

I was in a pretty sullen mood at home, too. I spent hours in my room, cursing the fates that were sending me up the creek—Blossom

Creek, to be precise. When Mom or Dad would ask me about school or my friends, I would answer in monosyllables. I guess I was pretty obnoxious, but the only consolation I had was feeling sorry for myself.

Dad was spending a lot of time down in Kentucky, leaving the responsibility of selling the house to Mom. She was in quite a state herself, finishing her current novel, trying to sell the house, and having to put up with my world-class sulks. I think she would have gone crazy except for fantasizing about our new home in the country.

Both she and Dad had a severe case of country fever, but I was a city girl, or at least a metro girl. Sure, I liked looking at pretty scenery on vacation, but I had no desire to *live* out in the sticks. I loved being so close to Chicago. You always felt you were part of an exciting and powerful world there, a world of movers and shakers. I doubted there was any moving and shaking going on in Blossom Creek.

School ended, and the real estate agent began leading hordes of people through our house. Dad's hopes of making a quick sale faded as the summer wore on and there were no takers, but as I hung out with my friends, my spirits began reviving. Maybe we wouldn't be able to sell the house at all. Then we'd have to stay, and I could go back to Glen Forest High. It would be a pain for Dad to keep flying back and forth from Kentucky, but surely he could do it until I graduated.

By August I felt I might luck out after all—until our real estate agent showed the house to a young couple with a little kid. The minute I saw them, I knew my luck had run out. The woman kept murmuring "I love it! It's perfect!" Her husband kept giving her dopey grins and nodding. As for the kid, he just kept whining, "When are we gonna eat?"

I was glad when they all departed so the little brat could feed his face. But all that evening I had a sinking feeling. Sure enough, at about nine the agent called, announcing that the couple would pay the asking price on our house.

I was crushed, but Mom was ecstatic and called Dad in Kentucky right away. Now, however, they were worried that they would have trouble finding a place near Blossom Creek before the month was out.

Then one night Dad phoned and I could see

that Mom was getting all excited as he spoke to her. "And it has a pond?" she asked, grinning from ear to ear. "Dogwoods and redbuds? The garden's already dug? Oh, Dick, it sounds wonderful!"

I couldn't take all the gushing, so I went into the kitchen, got a humongous bowl of mint chocolate chip ice cream to drown my sorrows, and went up to my room to listen to my favorite CDs.

Sometime later Mom knocked on my door. "Tess?" She came in and I gave her what must have been a glowering look, because she sighed and shook her head. "Aren't you ever going to get over this funk you're in? It's getting pretty tiresome."

"I guess I should be celebrating, right? You and Dad got exactly what you wanted, so that's just great," I said sarcastically.

"Tess, I really am sorry," Mom said. "We wish all this had happened after you graduated, but that's not how things worked out."

"Mom, it was going to be such a terrific year!" I moaned.

"I know, honey. It's a horrible disappointment after making Note-ables. But you can join the school chorus in Blossom Creek.

11

You're so smart, Tess, and so talented. You'll do well anywhere you go."

I was about to make some crack, but then I saw the eager look on Mom's face, and I didn't have the heart. Maybe I had been a little hard on her—after all, Dad was the one who was making us move.

I managed a feeble smile. "Don't worry, Mom. Blossom Creek probably won't be as horrible as I think it will be."

Mom smiled too. "That's a positive thought. And your father has found a really great place for us. . . ."

I tried to look interested as she began to tell me enthusiastically about all the wonders of our new Kentucky home, but I knew in my heart that I would positively hate it.

Chapter Two

The large moving van arrived at our house bright and early on a blistering hot August day. The movers hurried back and forth, carting out furniture and boxes in an amazing display of speed and efficiency. Dad's plan was to see the movers off, then start for Kentucky. That night we would stay in Louisville and reach our new house the next day.

At last the van pulled away. Tears welled up in my eyes, and I sniffled miserably. Flipping on my sunglasses, I took one last, sad look around and then quickly got into the backseat of the car.

"Well," said Dad, looking a little uncomfortable, "I guess it's time we hit the road."

In no time at all we were in Indiana on Interstate 65, heading south. We stopped for lunch in Indianapolis and made the final jaunt to Louisville in a couple of hours. That night we stayed in a luxury hotel overlooking the river. As I looked out the window at the lights twinkling across the bridge and at the looming buildings on the shore, I sighed. Maybe it wouldn't have been quite so bad if we had been moving to Louisville. After all, it was a city, even if it was a pretty small one. It was civilization with art and culture and shopping malls. But Blossom Creek? If I was lucky, it would probably have one run-down movie theater and a country store run by somebody named Floyd or something.

After breakfast the next morning we set out for Blossom Creek. The landscape soon became quite rolling and dotted with trees. There were a few scraggly-looking cornfields every so often and a number of fields with large, leafy green plants that Dad informed me were tobacco. Finally, the highway dipped into a large curve. Right up ahead was a water tower and buildings signifying a town. A sign proclaimed BLOSSOM CREEK, POP. 5200.

It was pretty much what I had expected. Oh, it did have a few signs of civilization, like the McDonald's on one corner and a video store on another. But mostly it was a rather shabby little town with what seemed to be an abnormally high number of pickup trucks on the main street.

"We'll stop and get some gas before we drive out to the place," Dad said. "I sure hope the movers are there by now."

He turned the car into a gas station and pulled up in front of the ancient-looking pumps. As he got out of the car, he added, "Tess, why don't you clean the windshield while I get the gas?"

Scowling, I got out and looked around, but couldn't find anything for cleaning windshields. "I guess they don't clean windshields in this town," I said sarcastically.

While Dad began to struggle with the pump, a rusted-out pickup blasting country music pulled up next to us and a bearded man in a tank top and cowboy hat got out. As he walked toward the gas station, he yelled to the woman in the truck, "Just corn curls, right, hon?"

The woman stuck her head out the window and yelled back, "Get me a Milky Way too, Curtis."

A minute later Curtis returned with his purchases, got into the pickup, and gunned it out of the lot.

"Dad," I said a little desperately, "why did you make us come here?"

He stopped fiddling with the pump and frowned at me. "Listen, Tess, you'll like it here, really. You've only been here about three minutes."

"Three centuries wouldn't make a difference," I cried. "I hate it! I'll always hate it! Blossom Creek is a total Hicksville!"

As soon as I said this, I got the horrible feeling that Dad wasn't the only person listening. Sure enough, when I glanced around, I saw a guy standing near us. He looked about my age, tall and thin, with unruly dark hair and blue eyes. Those eyes were regarding me with undisguised hostility, and I suddenly wished I could sink into the ground.

The guy brushed past me and went over to Dad. "Having trouble with the pump?" he asked in a soft drawl.

Dad nodded. "I can't seem to move the handle."

Giving the handle a good yank, the guy said, "It's been getting stuck lately." Then he walked back to the gas station.

Dad began to fill the tank. "You've certainly made a great first impression, Tess," he said quietly. "I'm sure that kid enjoyed hearing what a hick you think he is."

Feeling guilty, I climbed back into the car. "What was that all about?" Mom asked.

"Nothing," I muttered.

After Dad finished pumping the gas, he started toward the station and was met at the door by the dark-haired guy. I watched as the guy took Dad's money and gave him his change. He still had the same surly expression on his face, and when he glanced over at our car, I slid farther down into the seat.

A moment later Dad got in, turned the key in the ignition, and we were on our way again.

Our new home was located about six miles outside of town. As we drove down the highway, I tried to forget the guy at the gas station and concentrate on my new surroundings. I had to grudgingly admit that the countryside was beautiful. When we came to a rustic bridge over a wide stream, Dad said, "This is Blossom Creek. And see that rise up there on the right? That's our land."

Suddenly I had a curious sense of excitement. Now I was eager to see the place. As we drove along, I noticed wire fencing along the wooded roadside, punctuated every several yards by large Keep Out signs.

"Who lives here, Dad?" I asked. "They sure don't seem very friendly."

"I haven't met that neighbor," he told me. "She's an old woman named Mary McConnell, but around here she's known as Crazy Mary."

"Oh, great." I sighed. "So we're living next to a psychopath?"

"She's perfectly harmless," Dad said. "She's just a little eccentric, I guess. Lives by herself. She's something of a hermit."

"Little towns like Blossom Creek always have their characters, you know," Mom added.

The idea of living next to a hermit was pretty intriguing. I knew there was usually some tragic tale connected with people becoming hermits, and I was wondering what Crazy Mary's story was, when Dad interrupted my musings.

"This is it," he said proudly, turning the car into a narrow, winding drive. "We're on our land now."

We drove through a densely wooded area,

then past a meadow dotted with purple and yellow wildflowers. Beyond the meadow was a rambling farmhouse with a huge front porch, and behind the house were tree-laden hills. I was all prepared to hate my parents' country dream on sight, but I just couldn't. It was beautiful.

"It's—nice," I managed to say, and Dad and Mom smiled at each other.

Dad pulled up in front of the house and parked. "Well, c'mon, ladies. I'll give you the grand tour," he said.

The inside of the house was every bit as charming as the outside, with oak floors, big windows, and a wonderful curved wooden staircase.

"We thought this could be your room, Tess," Mom said as we approached a doorway at the end of the upstairs hall.

I walked into the large, sunny room and gazed out one of the windows at the pictur-esque view.

Dad gave me an eager look. "Well?'"

"Yeah, okay," I replied, trying to sound like it was no big deal. But I was already planning where I would put my things. At least I would be miserable in scenic surroundings, I thought.

Just then we heard the moving van pulling up outside, and I followed Mom and Dad downstairs to supervise the movers.

The next week and a half passed surprisingly quickly as we got everything in order. I also spent a lot of time on the phone, telling Melissa and a few of my other friends back home about my exile.

But I couldn't help starting to like the place. Still, I would soon have to face going to my new school and meeting the "natives," and as September approached, I dreaded it more and more. Mom and I had driven past the school one day on a run to the local grocery store. It was a fairly new brick building situated out in the country—not the run-down wreck I had expected, but it was no Glen Forest High, that was for sure.

Dad spent most of Labor Day weekend at the new plant. Mom was holed up in her upstairs study, typing away on her computer at a frenzied pace, so I was pretty much on my own, and feeling sorrier for myself by the minute. Not even playing the guitar helped me to forget that I was separated from my friends, my home, my music, everything that really mattered to me.

On Monday I decided to take a walk, hoping it would cheer me up. I went down the path to the pond behind the house, then started wandering along a narrow dirt road by the side of an overgrown pasture. Coming to a wooded area, I noticed a small path leading into the trees. As I followed it, feeling like an explorer in the wilderness, I suddenly saw something interesting.

High in the crotch of a tall oak was a structure that looked very much like a tree house. It was just a sad-looking wooden platform with a few side boards, and windows cut through, but I could imagine that a long time ago it must have been some kid's pride and joy.

Walking over to the tree, I awkwardly climbed up the boarded footings that had been nailed to the trunk. When I reached the platform, I lay down on my back and gazed up into the branches. The sun glinted through the green and I smiled, remembering the willow tree in the backyard of our old house.

Suddenly I heard a noise. Peering out through one of the windows, I saw a huge, jowly brown dog snuffling along the path. It stopped at the base of my tree, pawed at the trunk, and gave a loud howl.

"Samson!" cried a voice. "What are you up to?"

I watched as an elderly woman in jeans and a loose-fitting white shirt came into view. She was tall and sturdy-looking, and her long gray hair resembled a messy bird's nest.

"What poor varmint have you treed this time, you bad dog?" she growled affectionately, glancing up at the tree house.

I sat up and looked over the side. "Hi," I said. "I guess I'm the varmint."

The woman looked both surprised and angry. "What are you doing up there? Get down right this minute!"

I clumsily climbed down the trunk. As soon as I reached the ground, the dog began sniffing me.

"Get away from her, Samson," the woman ordered gruffly, and after one last sniff the dog slunk over to his mistress. Then, scowling at me, the woman said, "Don't you know this is private property?"

"I live here," I said somewhat defensively. "I was just . . ."

"What do you mean, you live here?" she

snapped. "This is my property, and I don't like kids prowling around, causing trouble."

By now I had figured out that the woman must be Crazy Mary, and I sure hoped Dad was right about her being harmless. "I'm not causing trouble. And I thought this was *our* property," I said nervously. "I'm Tess Lawrence. We just moved into the house back there." I waved in the general direction of the farmhouse.

"You mean the old Sellers place?"

I nodded. "I'm sorry if I'm trespassing. I was just out walking and I saw the tree house and—well, I just thought I'd climb up to it. I know I'm a little old for that, but it sort of reminded me of a tree back home. I mean, my willow tree didn't have a tree house, but it had these long branches you could hide under and—" I stopped, realizing that I had started to babble. "I guess it sounds really dumb, being homesick for a tree."

The woman's expression suddenly softened. "Homesick for a tree?" she repeated. "No, it doesn't sound dumb at all." As she glanced up at the tree house, she didn't look mean anymore, just sort of defeated and sad. Then she turned back to me. "I'm sorry I carried on so.

It's just that I've had kids come around playing tricks. I thought you were one of them. I'm your neighbor, Mary McConnell." Indicating the dog, she added, "And this here is Samson."

I bent down to scratch his huge head, and Samson grinned from ear to ear. "Hi, Samson," I said, then asked, "What kind of dog is he?"

"Mostly bloodhound, I reckon. I got him when he was just a pup. His owner didn't think he had the makings of a tracker, so he was going to put him down."

Horrified, I asked, "You mean kill him?"

Mrs. McConnell nodded. "Some people think a dog that can't hunt got no right to live." Samson snuffled back over to her and she petted him. "Yes, you're a good old dog, Sammy."

"I'm glad you saved him," I said, smiling.

The old woman smiled back, much to my surprise. "Well, I guess Samson and me better be getting back." She turned to leave, then paused and said over her shoulder, "Oh, and you can come here to this old tree anytime you want."

"Thanks, Mrs. McConnell," I said.

The old woman and her dog disappeared down the wooded path. I decided I'd better get home too, so I started off in the opposite direction. As I walked back toward the house, I wondered about Mrs. McConnell. I realized that I hadn't even asked her whose tree house it had been.

Chapter Three

The day of doom arrived and I stood in front of my closet, trying to decide what to wear to school. After pulling out and discarding several outfits, I finally settled on a denim skirt and an embroidered white peasant blouse.

Looking into my dresser mirror, I decided I looked pretty decent. Although I'm far from being a knockout, I'm not too bad-looking. The best thing I have going for me is my hair. It's reddish-brown—auburn, I guess you'd call it—and it's nice and thick with a bit of curl to it.

After taking one last look in the mirror, I grabbed my huge canvas shoulder bag and made my way downstairs. Dad had already gone to work and Mom was at the kitchen table, reading the newspaper and drinking a cup of coffee. She looked up at me as I came in and smiled.

"You look nice, Tess," she said. "Are you nervous?"

I dropped my bag on the floor and sank down into a chair. "Me, nervous? Just because I'm going to a new school filled with strangers who talk funny? I'm not nervous—I'm terrified!"

Mom patted my hand reassuringly as she stood up. "I know it's hard, honey, but after about ten minutes I'm sure you'll feel right at home. Now, what would you like for breakfast?"

"I'm not hungry," I muttered. "In fact, I think I just might throw up."

But I finally agreed to a glass of orange juice and a toasted bagel. As I nibbled the bagel, I kept my eyes glued to the clock. At last I sighed and said, "I guess we'd better get going."

Mom nodded. "You certainly don't want to be late on your very first day at Blossom Creek High. Now, you have your schedule, right? And those forms you're supposed to turn in at the office first thing?"

"Yes, Mom, I've got everything," I assured her. I picked up my bag and followed her out the door.

We drove in silence to the school. When we pulled up in front of the building, I saw a mob of kids standing around the grounds in small groups, laughing and talking. The sight made me feel even sicker. I didn't belong in any of those groups. I was an alien, an outsider, and worse yet, a Yankee. They would all probably think *I* talked funny!

Mom smiled encouragingly at me as I got out of the car. "Good luck," she said.

"Thanks. I have a feeling I'm going to need it," I replied.

I watched as she pulled away, giving me a cheery little wave. *Sure, it's fine for her,* I thought. *Mom's headed back to the fantasy world of her new romance novel,* Destiny and Desire, *but I'm stuck in the real world of Blossom Creek High.* Sighing, I started walking past the groups of kids, heading for the front doors of the school.

It wasn't hard finding the office, since it was right inside the main entrance. Kids were already milling around the halls and some teacher types were hurrying somewhere, probably to the teachers' lounge for a last-minute cup of strong coffee before facing their classes. I hadn't gotten to school all that early, and I wondered if I'd have any time to explore the place before class began.

I stepped inside the office door and was dismayed to find a line in front of the counter. A middle-aged woman seemed to be the only person behind the counter, and she seemed to be moving things along as slowly as her drawled speech. Then I saw a short blond girl at a desk in a corner of the office. She was stapling stacks of various-colored paper together, and every so often she'd glance over at the crowd with an amused expression on her round face.

I waited—and waited, and waited. Just as the last kid in front of me left and it was finally my turn, the woman said, " 'Scuse me a second, hon," and disappeared inside a door at the back of the office. I couldn't believe it! I guess I must have looked really outraged, because the girl doing the stapling laughed.

"Don't worry, Mrs. Landers will be right back," she said. She left the stack of papers on the desk and came over to the counter. "I think she went to the ladies'. Maybe I can help you."

The blond girl was regarding me with such a

friendly smile that I couldn't help smiling back. "Thanks," I said. "You see, I'm new, and I was supposed to leave these forms . . ."

"From the way you talk, I can tell you're not from around here," the girl said. "Welcome to B.C. High. Where are y'all from?"

"Glen Forest. It's a suburb north of Chicago—" I began.

"Chicago? No kidding!" She seemed very impressed. "I was in Chicago last summer to visit my brother Buddy. He's in the navy, stationed at Great Lakes. So what are y'all doing here?"

"My father was transferred to Blossom Creek," I told her. "He's in charge of the new Cookie Crumbles factory, and—"

"Hey, that's cool!" the girl interrupted. Apparently I was never going to be allowed to finish a sentence. She looked down at the forms I'd handed her. "So you're Tess Lawrence. Well, Tess, I sure hope you like it here. I'm Lenny— Lenny Harris."

I must have looked puzzled, because she laughed and said, "I know—what kind of a dumb name is that for a girl, right? It's actually Lenore. *Lenore!* Can you think of anything more putrid?"

I laughed too. "I've heard worse. Hi, Lenny. Nice to meet you."

She looked down at my papers again. "There's no problem with this stuff—it's just the usual red tape. I'll give the forms to Mrs. Landers as soon as she gets back. Do you have your schedule?"

I nodded and pulled it out of the folder I'd brought with me. Lenny studied it intently. "Hey, you're a junior too! It looks like you're in my afternoon English and P.E. classes, and you signed up for chorus. That's great! We need all the voices we can get. Now, let's see— you'll need a locker . . ."

Lenny went over to a filing cabinet and opened a drawer. After fishing around for a while, she took a piece of paper out of a folder and came back to me. "Here you go—this is the combination to locker number 263. That's up on the second floor, near the music room. Know where that is?"

I shook my head. "I don't know where *any-thing* is. I've never been inside the school until right now. I registered by mail."

"Well then, why don't I take you to it? I guess we don't have time for the grand tour, but I can show you your locker and point out the general layout of the place."

Just then Mrs. Landers came back into the office. "Sorry, hon," she said, smiling maternally at me. "Now, what can I do for you?"

Before I could answer, Lenny said, "This is Tess Lawrence, Mrs. L. She's new." Thrusting my papers at the woman, she added, "And here are her registration forms. I gave her her locker information and now I'm going to show her where it is."

"But Lenny, what about the stapling?" Mrs. Landers asked.

"All done," Lenny informed her. "Everything's on the desk over there." Turning to me, she said, "C'mon, Tess, let's get a move on!"

She dashed out of the office and I rushed after her. When we were in the hallway, Lenny grinned at me. "I thought we'd better scoot before Mrs. L. starts going over your papers. She would have taken forever."

Lenny led the way down the crowded corridor and up the stairs. As I followed her, I was beginning to feel a little better, even though it was kind of disconcerting to be surrounded by the constant chatter of southern accents.

When we reached the second floor, Lenny

pointed out where a couple of my classes would be, and then directed me to my locker. It was in what appeared to be a major thoroughfare. There wasn't much room as streams of kids noisily made their way past us.

"Why don't you try the combination just to make sure it works?" Lenny suggested. "These locks are pretty old, and sometimes they get fouled up."

Taking out the slip of paper she had given me, I carefully worked the combination, but nothing happened. I tried again, yanking at the door so hard that my shoulder bag slipped down my arm.

"Looks like it's stuck," Lenny said cheerfully, and gave the locker door a whack with her fist. "There. Try it now."

I yanked again, but it still wouldn't budge. My bulky bag was in the way, so I put it down on the floor behind me and gave the door one last pull. This time it opened.

"All right!" Lenny cheered.

As I gazed into the empty locker, wondering about all the other kids who had used it before me, I was dimly aware of a tall guy rushing past me. He suddenly stumbled and went careening toward the opposite wall, crashing loudly into the bank of lockers there. Some kids who were passing by laughed and clapped and someone shouted loudly, "Way to go, Stoddard!"

Lenny looked down at the floor and giggled. "I think he tripped over your bag, Tess," she said.

I followed her gaze and saw that my shoulder bag was now in the middle of the hallway. I quickly bent down and picked it up, turning to the guy who had stumbled.

"I'm so sorry . . ." I began, and then stopped in surprise. It was the same guy who had been at the gas station on the day I had arrived in Blossom Creek, and he was staring at me with the same hostile expression.

"Why do you girls always have to carry suitcases around with you?" he growled.

"Oh, c'mon, Luke. Lighten up," Lenny said. "It's no big deal."

He just scowled at her, gave me one last withering look, and stalked away.

"He seemed awfully mad at me," I murmured nervously.

Lenny shrugged. "Don't mind him. It's not just you—Luke has a grudge against the world."

Her comment intrigued me, and I was about to ask her to explain, when a shrill buzzer sounded.

"Oops—that's the first bell," Lenny said. "Your chemistry class is at the far end of the first floor, so we'd better get it in gear or we're both going to be late."

We rushed down the stairway. I was a little breathless by the time we stopped in front of a door in the now practically deserted corridor.

"This is the chem lab, Tess," Lenny told me. "Good luck! I'll catch you later, okay?"

She hurried off, and I squared my shoulders, took a deep breath, and opened the class-room door.

The second bell rang as I entered. I paused on the threshold, facing a room full of kids, and a short, pudgy man with a crew cut who I figured must be the chemistry teacher, Mr. Todd. They were all staring at me with great interest. I couldn't have been more conspicuous if I had tried!

Mr. Todd smiled at me. "Well, young lady, you made it just under the wire. Another second and you would have been in big trouble, Miss . . . ?"

"Lawrence," I mumbled. "Tess Lawrence."

He nodded, then looked over the class. "Let's see—you'll need a lab partner . . ."

There were two kids seated at each lab table. It appeared that the whole class was filled up, but then I saw one empty seat just as Mr. Todd said briskly, "Luke Stoddard, you now have a partner."

I stared in dismay at the boy sitting at the table with the empty seat. It was the guy from the gas station who had just tripped over my bag! The teacher turned to me and said, "Tess, please take that seat at the back of the last row."

I nodded numbly and made my way past the rows of unfamiliar, smiling faces. When I reached Luke's table, I sat down and very carefully tucked my bag under my chair. Then I shot a quick sideways glance at my new lab partner. He just stared straight ahead, as if I weren't even there.

During Mr. Todd's lecture I kept sneaking peeks at Luke, who regarded the teacher with an impassive expression on his face. I remembered what Lenny had said about his having a grudge against the world, and once again I wondered what she meant by that.

When class was over I decided to say something friendly to him. But just as I started to speak, a boy at the table in front of ours turned around. When he smiled at me, I was just about bowled over. I had never in my whole life seen such a gorgeous guy—except for Michael Wright, of course. He was tall and very well built, with sandy blond hair and hazel eyes.

"Hi, Tess," he said in a deep, resonant voice. "You're new here, right? I'm Carter Davis." He motioned to the boy next to him. "And this is my pal, Brad Robinson." Brad, who was stocky and somewhat shorter than Carter, nodded.

"Uh—hi," I murmured, smiling at them both.

"Boy, Stoddard, you get all the luck," Carter said to Luke. "How'd you manage to get Tess for a lab partner while I'm stuck with old Brad?"

Brad punched his arm. "What's the matter? Don't you love me anymore?"

Carter punched him back. "Cut it out, you moron!"

Luke didn't say a word. He just stood up and, scowling, made his way to the door.

Turning back to me, Carter said, "Your father must be in charge of the new Cookie Crumbles factory. My dad mentioned meeting him a while ago, and the name rang a bell. I hope you're going to like it here, Tess."

"Yeah," Brad added. "We're not so bad when you get to know us."

I stood up, smiling at them both. "It's been nice meeting you, but I'd better get going to my next class. I don't want to be late—or almost late—again."

Carter's answering smile made me weak in the knees. "We certainly wouldn't want that. What's your next class?"

Checking my schedule, I replied, "Algebra with Mrs. Miller."

Carter and Brad shook their heads dolefully. "So you've got her, too." Brad sighed.

"That sounds ominous," I said, feeling apprehensive.

"Better believe it." Carter stood and so did Brad. "C'mon—we're headed that way. We'll give you moral support."

As the three of us left the classroom, I thought that there certainly was something to southern hospitality—except for notable exceptions like Luke Stoddard. But then Carter asked me a question, and I forgot all about Luke, at least for the moment.

Chapter Four

The rest of the morning was fairly painless. Although I didn't have an opportunity to meet many other kids, they all seemed friendly enough. Except, of course, for Luke Stoddard.

Unfortunately, it turned out that Luke was in every single one of my morning classes, appearing like a dark cloud in a sunlit sky. I had to admit I was curious about him, though. I kept wondering why he had a grudge against the world, and as the morning progressed, I came up with several theories about Luke that would have made perfect soap opera plots.

When the bell rang for lunch, I followed a

mob of kids to the cafeteria. After paying for my food, I glanced anxiously around at the tables, trying to figure out where to sit. There are few lonelier feelings than standing with your tray in a cafeteria full of strangers, all of whom are completely preoccupied with their food and their friends.

Then all of a sudden I heard someone call my name. It was Lenny. She was sitting at a table with two other girls, and when she caught my eye, she motioned for me to join them.

I hurried over to her table, and Lenny greeted me like an old pal. She quickly introduced me to the girls, and since I recognized them from my chemistry and algebra classes, we already had some common ground.

Sandra Martin said, "I noticed Carter talking to you after chemistry, Tess."

"Boy, are you lucky!" Dawn Ritter sighed. "He's never said a word to me."

"I don't know why you think Carter's so great, Dawn," Lenny said, frowning. "He's so stuck on himself, it's sickening."

Dawn seemed to take this as a personal insult. "Oh, Lenny, he is not! I think he's sweet. And he's *so* cute!"

"So he's good-looking," Lenny said with a shrug. "So what? If you ask me, Carter Davis is nothing but a big jerk. Just because his family's rich and his father's a judge, he thinks he's hot stuff. And his sister's every bit as conceited as he is."

Just as Dawn was about to launch into a heated defense of her idol, Carter himself turned up at our table with his sidekick, Brad Robinson. "Hi, ladies," he said, giving us all one of those dazzling smiles. "Y'all look like you're having a serious discussion here. Trying to solve all the world's problems?"

Dawn blushed and giggled, but I could see that Lenny wasn't amused. "Yeah, right," she said sarcastically. "And I guess you and Brad have been talking about the situation in the Middle East."

"Heck no," Carter said, laughing. "We were talking about girls."

Dawn giggled again, but Carter ignored her, turning his attention to me instead. "So, Tess, how's it going?"

I smiled. "Okay so far. I'm surviving, anyway."

"That's good. Too bad you got stuck with Stoddard in chemistry, though."

"Oh, lay off, Carter," Lenny snapped. "There's

nothing wrong with Luke. He's just had a rough time, that's all."

Carter shrugged his broad shoulders. "Yeah, I know he's had a rough time, but he doesn't have to take it out on everybody else. Besides, Stoddard always was kind of strange, even before the thing with his old man."

I was hoping he would say more about Luke, but just then a female voice called Carter's name. Looking around, I saw a pretty, dark-haired girl waving at him.

Carter looked a little annoyed, but he said to me, "Well, guess I'll talk to you later, Tess. Take care now."

I watched as he walked off to join the girl, followed by Brad, his silent shadow. When I turned back to the table, I saw Dawn regarding me with a wistful expression.

"Wow, Tess, Carter must really like you," she said sadly. "He sure was paying a lot of attention to you."

Sandy grinned. "Yeah, Tess, you better watch out. Ol' Carter is quite the ladies' man."

"What do you mean, watch out?" Dawn said. "I'd just love it if Carter showed some interest in *me*!"

42

Lenny just shot her an exasperated look and shook her head.

Deciding to change the subject, I asked Lenny, "What did you mean about Luke Stoddard having a rough time?"

"Well," Lenny said, "last winter Luke's daddy was playing over in Cedarville, and—"

"Playing?" I asked, puzzled. "Playing what?"

"Oh, I forgot—you don't know that Charlie Stoddard was a musician, one of the best fiddle players in Kentucky," Lenny said.

"But a lot of people think Luke's even better," Dawn added. "The whole family's musical—except for Luke's mother, that is. Luke, his daddy, and his four brothers had a band. They were known as The Stompin' Stoddards."

I hadn't failed to notice that she and Lenny were speaking in the past tense. "What happened?" I asked.

"Well, like I said before, Luke's daddy was playing alone over at Cedarville one night last winter," Lenny replied. "It was a school night and Mrs. Stoddard didn't want the kids to go out. Anyway, Charlie went and had himself a good time like he usually did." She paused. "You see, Charlie Stoddard had a drinking problem. And—well, on the way home he drove his pickup into a tree and was killed instantly."

I gasped. "How awful!"

All three girls nodded solemnly. "It sure was," Lenny said. "It's been real rough on Luke and his mother. The Stoddards have always been hard up, and now with Luke's father gone it's even worse. I don't think he left much of anything for his family. I imagine it's tough making ends meet. A lot of the responsibility falls on Luke, him being the oldest and all."

"Yeah," Sandra said. "I think that's why he acts the way he does. He's got an awful lot on his mind, and he works real hard. I guess the rest of us seem pretty immature and silly to him."

A wave of sympathy flooded me as I listened to Luke Stoddard's sad story, and I shuddered as I thought about my own father and how terrible it would be if something happened to him.

The harsh sound of the bell brought me back to reality.

"Come on, Tess," Lenny said as we all stood and picked up our trays. "We're in the same English class. Let's hurry so we can get some decent seats."

As I followed her out of the cafeteria, I was still thinking about Luke Stoddard. I kept on thinking about him as Lenny and I snagged two desks near the back of the classroom. Shortly after we had taken our seats, Luke entered the room and sat down at the desk right across from mine. On impulse I looked straight at him and said hello.

Luke looked surprised. "Hi," he muttered.

"Listen," I said quickly before he could turn away, "I just want to tell you that I'm sorry I tripped you this morning. Or my *bag* tripped you, I mean. It really was dumb putting it on the floor like that, but I was trying to get my locker open and it wouldn't budge and my bag was getting in the way . . ." *You're babbling, Tess,* I told myself, and broke off abruptly.

To my relief, I saw a glint of amusement in Luke's blue eyes. "That's okay," he said in his soft drawl. "It wasn't your fault. I'm sorry I was so rude and all."

Pleased by his unexpected apology, I smiled at him. To my surprise, Luke smiled back. It was amazing how that smile transformed him. He didn't look like the same Luke Stoddard.

Since we were getting on so well, I decided to continue the conversation. "I understand you're a musician. That's really neat."

45

Instantly Luke's smile disappeared and his eyes narrowed suspiciously. "How'd you know that?" he asked.

"Oh, somebody just happened to mention it at lunch," I said, feeling suddenly awkward and uncomfortable. I was trying desperately to think of something else to say, when Carter Davis came up beside me.

"Hi, Tess," he said with his usual charming smile. "Is the desk in front of you taken?"

"No—I mean, I don't think so," I muttered.

"Great!" As Carter lowered his tall, athletic frame into the seat, he said, "So we're in another class together. Must be fate, huh?" He was giving me such an unmistakably flirtatious look that I felt myself blushing.

"Must be," I agreed.

Just then the teacher, Ms. Wallace, came in, and after winking at me, Carter turned around and focused his attention on her. I glanced over at Luke, who had that familiar surly expression on his face again as he listened to Ms. Wallace discuss the outline for the course.

For the rest of the period I tried to concentrate on what the teacher was saying, but I couldn't get Luke Stoddard out of my mind.

* * *

At last my first day at B.C. High was coming to an end and Lenny and I were on our way to chorus. Lenny had told me that the Blossom Creek Chorus was pretty pathetic, and it didn't take me long to find out how right she was.

After entering the somewhat cramped music room, we joined a couple of other girls Lenny knew. I looked around in surprise when the bell rang. There were only about twenty kids in the room, and only two of them were boys.

"Where is everybody?" I whispered to Lenny.

"This is it, Tess," she whispered back. "Don't say I didn't warn you."

"But there are only two guys," I protested.

"Yeah—Kevin Horner and Ben Williams. Ben's pretty good, but Kevin sings like a bad Wayne Newton."

I giggled. "Is there a *good* one?" Looking around again, I noticed a tall, attractive blonde talking with a small group of girls. "Who's that?" I asked Lenny.

Lenny made a face. "That's Carly Davis, Carter's sister. She's a senior, and a real pain in the neck. Carly's the star singer of the B.C. Chorus—in her own opinion anyway."

I studied Carly with interest, noting the resemblance to Carter now that Lenny had told me they were related. A moment later a short man bustled into the room. He had a pencil-thin mustache, and his dark hair was combed from the back of his head to the front.

"That's Mr. Cassin, the chorus director," Lenny whispered to me.

"Okay, gang," Mr. Cassin said in the standard Blossom Creek twang. He walked over to the piano, then looked around at the faces and shook his head. "I'm glad to see that my recruiting efforts paid off so dramatically," he added dryly.

"We do have one new person, Mr. Cassin," Lenny said, indicating me. "Tess Lawrence. She just moved here from Chicago."

The director's eyebrows shot up. "Really? Well, Miss Lawrence, what persuaded you to join us? Was it bribery or blackmail?"

All the kids laughed at this, and I grinned. "Neither, Mr. Cassin. I just like to sing, and I was in chorus at my school back home."

Mr. Cassin smiled. "Good. Glad to have you with us. Now, let's get warmed up on a few songs, and then I'll have each of you try out your voice a little."

One of the girls began passing out ancient

songbooks. When I got my copy, I looked down at the tattered pages with dismay, thinking wistfully of the piles of brand-new music we used to get at Glen Forest High.

"All right, ladies and gentlemen," the director said, sitting down at the piano and striking a chord. "Page twenty-four, if you please."

I turned to page twenty-four and found "Danny Boy." *Oh, brother,* I thought to myself. *What a clinker! At Glen Forest we wouldn't have been caught dead singing anything as old-fashioned as this.*

But oddly enough, once we started singing I realized that it wasn't all that bad. In fact, it was really beautiful, and the Blossom Creek Chorus did a fairly decent job on it, although I heard some pretty weird high notes coming from the soprano section.

After we had run through the song once, Mr. Cassin turned to me. "Miss Lawrence, how about showing us what you can do? Sing it from the beginning, will you?"

I swallowed hard. The last thing I wanted to do was sing a solo in front of all those kids whose eyes were now focused on me, but I couldn't very well refuse. So I tried to forget about everything but the music, and as Mr.

Cassin accompanied me on the piano, I sang "Danny Boy" as best I could.

When I finished, the director looked at me and grinned broadly. "Wonderful!" he exclaimed. "Miss Lawrence, that was absolutely *wonderful!*"

Everyone broke into applause then, and I felt myself blushing. As the clapping died away, Lenny leaned over to me and whispered, "Gee, Tess, I didn't know you had such a terrific voice!" She poked me in the ribs. "Look at Carly—she's fit to be tied!"

I glanced over at Carly Davis. There was no doubt about it—she did have a frosty expression on her pretty face, and I hoped I hadn't made an enemy of Carter's sister.

The period ended in what seemed like no time at all. As Lenny and I headed for the door, Mr. Cassin beamed at me. When we were outside in the hallway, Lenny said, "Did you see the way Cassin was looking at you? You'd think a Metropolitan Opera star had just joined the chorus!"

As she spoke, Carly Davis brushed past us, nose in the air. Grinning, Lenny watched her strut down the hall. "I think she looks a little green, don't you? There's no way Carly will be getting all the solos from now on!" She giggled. "Serves her right for being such a snob."

Lenny talked to me for several more minutes about the chorus, until she realized that she was about to miss her bus and dashed off down the hall.

As I walked down the stairs, a few kids I'd met that day said "Hi, Tess," and "See you tomorrow." I was smiling when I went outside and scanned the street for my mom's little red sports car. I found it near the entrance to the school parking lot, and as I approached it, I suddenly spotted Luke Stoddard in the lot, getting into the most beat-up pickup truck I'd ever seen.

Chorus had temporarily put Luke out of my mind, but as I walked toward Mom's car, I started remembering everything I'd learned about him and his family, and how hard up they were. It just didn't seem fair.

"Hi, honey," Mom said as I got into the car. "How did it go today?"

"Okay. It wasn't nearly as bad as I was afraid it would be," I replied, fastening my seat belt. "And don't you *dare* say I told you so!" I added with a grin.

Mom just smiled and turned the key in the

ignition. Before she could pull away from the curb, Luke Stoddard drove out of the parking lot. He looked directly at me, and I could tell he was taking in Mom's flashy little car. I gave him a smile and a little wave, but Luke didn't smile. His only response was a curt nod before he drove off down the street.

"Who was that grim-looking character, Tess?" Mom asked.

I shrugged. "Oh, just a guy who's in some of my classes," I said. Then I started telling her about my first day at B.C. High.

Chapter Five

Needless to say, I lived through the rest of my first week at Blossom Creek High. In fact, it was really weird because by the end of that week it seemed as if I had been there for months. My classes were okay and a few, like chemistry and English, were actually enjoyable. Of course, chorus turned out to be the highlight of each day. Maybe Mr. Cassin combed his hair funny, but he was really terrific, and although he was serious about music, he also believed in having fun with it. Best of all, I was getting to know a lot of the kids at school. Lenny had rapidly become a good friend, and I enjoyed hanging out with her and her gang.

I was also getting a lot of attention from gorgeous Carter Davis, which was flattering since most of the girls (except Lenny) were nuts about him. Lenny had told me that Carter had a current steady—Diana Webber, the girl who had waved at him in the cafeteria my first day. But according to Lenny, "current" for Carter could be measured in hours, and she warned me that Diana's days were numbered because Carter was definitely making a move on me. Although I thought that was pretty unlikely, he *did* seem to turn up wherever I happened to be.

Still, for some reason I couldn't stop thinking about Luke Stoddard. Maybe it was the old Tess Lawrence imagination going into overdrive, but I conjured up a pathetic picture of the dirt-poor Stoddard family dressed in rags and holed up in some awful shack. My imagination was all I had to rely on since I couldn't find out anything from Luke himself. All week he hardly spoke to me at all.

When I said something to Lenny about it, she said, "Luke's the quiet type. I guess he takes more after his mama than his daddy. His daddy was always the life of the party—you know, real loud and boisterous. I've known Luke since first grade and he's always been serious, like he's got all the worries of the world on his shoulders."

I wanted to learn more, but I noticed that Lenny was giving me a kind of curious look, like why was I so interested in Luke Stoddard anyway? So I changed the subject and didn't ask her about him again, even though I was dying to find out more about him. I didn't want Lenny to get the wrong idea. I mean, it wasn't as if I were romantically interested in Luke or anything.

When Saturday rolled around I called Melissa and told her all about my first week at school. She was glad it didn't sound as horrible as I'd feared, and then she told me everything that was going on at Glen Forest. I was surprised to discover that even hearing about the exciting program Note-ables were working on for their next concert didn't upset me very much. And after we hung up, although I felt a little homesick, I wasn't particularly depressed. I guess I was making progress.

For the rest of the morning I practiced my guitar. Then, since Dad was spending the entire day at the factory, Mom and I had lunch. After lunch Mom went back to working on her novel. I decided it was much too nice a day to stay indoors, so I started out on a hike around the pond, taking my paperback copy of *Pride and Prejudice* with me. We were reading it in English and I thought it would be pleasant to find a nice shady spot somewhere to share with Elizabeth Bennett and Mr. Darcy. *Pride and Prejudice* is without a doubt my absolute favorite book. I think Elizabeth is just great, and as for Mr. Darcy, he's quite a guy even though he seems to be an awful snob at first.

As I walked along, I remembered my previous hike when I had met our "hermit" neighbor, Mrs. McConnell. I'd been so preoccupied with school that I hadn't really thought much about her since then. When I got to the tree house, I looked around, almost expecting Samson to come snuffling through the trees again, but the woods were deserted.

The tree house seemed like an old friend to me and, tucking my book under my arm, I climbed up the tree and onto the wooden platform. Leaning back against the side of the tree house, I began to read and soon got caught up in the story. We were only supposed to read two chapters for class on Monday, but I didn't want to stop, so I kept on reading for some time.

I was surprised when I finally looked at my watch and saw that it was almost four o'clock. Deciding that it was time to go home, I tucked the book under my arm again and started to back off the platform. I hugged the tree trunk and felt around with one foot, trying to find the first plank. When my foot finally rested on it, I gingerly lowered my other foot. Just as I did this, the piece of board gave way and I started to fall. There was barely time for me to feel a moment of panic before I hit the ground, landing heavily on my left leg. A sharp jab of pain shot through my ankle, making me gasp.

I carefully stretched my left leg out in front of me and tried to wiggle my foot. The ankle still hurt a bit, but the pain wasn't excruciating. I waited a few minutes and then tried to stand up. As soon as I put my weight on my left foot, I felt a really awful pain and I crumpled to the ground.

Great, Tess, I thought to myself. *Now you've done it!*

I looked around and realized there was little chance of anyone finding me there. *Well, maybe Mom will come looking for me in a couple of hours,* I thought mournfully.

On the off chance that somebody might hear, I started yelling, "Help! Help!"

Suddenly I heard rustling and snorting sounds at the edge of the woods. I stiffened, half expecting Sasquatch to come lumbering toward me. Imagine my relief when I saw Mrs. McConnell's dog Samson trotting along the path! He saw me too, and stopped abruptly, raising his huge head and sniffing the air. Then he galloped over to me, howling in excitement.

I patted him and smiled. "Well, hello there!" I said. The dog began licking my face with his long pink tongue and I couldn't help laughing. "That tickles, Sammy! Cut it out!"

The dog stopped licking and stared at me with a questioning expression on his jowly face. "Isn't your mistress with you?" I asked, peering past him toward the path. But there was no sign of Mrs. McConnell. Turning back to Samson, I said, "Well, what do we do now?" The bloodhound cocked his head. "Lassie would have some idea by now," I informed him, but Samson just grinned idiotically.

Then I had a sudden inspiration. Grabbing

the paperback I'd dropped when I fell, I said eagerly, "Listen, Sammy! Take this book back to your mistress. She'll have to investigate when you turn up with a copy of *Pride and Prejudice* in your mouth!"

But Samson didn't seem to get the message. I sighed. "Well, it was just an idea. I guess someone will come eventually. . . ."

I looked down at my ankle. It hurt a lot more now, and I could see that it was swollen and turning black and blue. I was just wondering if maybe I could crawl down the path on my hands and knees, when I heard a voice calling, "Samson! Samson, where are you?"

"Mrs. McConnell!" I shouted. "It's Tess Lawrence! Samson's here with me. I need help!"

The dog jumped up and raced toward the path. When Mrs. McConnell appeared, he rushed over to her with a long, loud howl of welcome.

Mrs. McConnell saw me at once and hurried to my side. "What happened, Tess?" she asked.

"I climbed up into the tree house again," I told her sheepishly, "and I'm afraid I fell climbing down and hurt my ankle. Pretty dumb, huh?"

The old woman crouched down next to me, studying my ankle with a concerned look on her face. She gently felt it and then frowned. "I don't think anything's broken, but you'd better have a doctor look at it," she said. "My house is close by. Do you think you can make it if you lean on me?"

"I'll try," I said.

I managed to stand up, putting all my weight on my good leg. Mrs. McConnell put an arm around me and I put one hand on her shoulder. Very slowly we made our way out of the woods and down the path with me kind of hopping on one foot. We passed a small orchard, and beyond it a large garden. On the other side of the garden was a small white house.

When we got to the porch, a big orange tabby cat blinked at us. Samson gave her a disdainful sniff and followed us into the house, through the kitchen, and down a hall to the living room. Mrs. McConnell maneuvered me to an old couch covered with a crocheted afghan, and I sank gratefully down on it.

"Prop your foot up on the couch," she said. I did, with a grimace of pain. "We'd better get that shoe off," Mrs. McConnell muttered, carefully loosening the laces of my running shoe and removing it from my foot. Then she left the room and hurried back a moment later with a bag of ice. "Here—this might help take down the swelling a bit."

"Thanks, Mrs. McConnell," I said, placing the bag against my ankle. "Could you call my mom so she can come and get me?"

"I'd be glad to, but I don't have a phone," Mrs. McConnell said. I was so amazed that I just stared at her. I couldn't imagine anyone not having a phone, not even in Blossom Creek!

"I'll go over to your house and tell your mother what's happened," she went on. "I won't be long. Samson'll stay with you."

Without another word Mrs. McConnell walked briskly out of the room. Samson, looking very sorrowful at being left behind, heaved a huge sigh and lay down beside the couch.

"Don't worry, Sammy. She'll be right back," I assured him.

The ice seemed to be helping my ankle, and as I waited, I looked around the room for the first time. It was small and sparsely furnished, with a few flower prints on the walls. Next to the couch was a rocking chair and a small table with an old-fashioned lamp and a couple of framed photographs on it. I managed to scoot myself over to the table and turned the large picture frame toward me.

I saw what appeared to be a high school graduation picture of a boy who I decided must be Mrs. McConnell's son. He had her same broad features, and was looking at the camera with a slightly wary, uncomfortable look. Then I picked up the other picture. It was the same boy, except in this photograph he was a lot younger. He had his arms around the two hound dogs sitting on either side of him, and all three of them had wide grins on their faces.

I studied the picture for some time, realizing that the boy in the picture must have been the owner of the tree house. Smiling, I put the picture frame back on the table.

It wasn't long before I heard a car pull up in front of the house. Mrs. McConnell came through the door, followed by both Dad and Mom.

"Baby, are you okay?" Dad asked anxiously as he and Mom hurried over to me. I knew he was worried, because he hardly ever calls me "baby" anymore—I usually won't let him. But under the circumstances, I let it pass.

"Yeah, I'm okay, Dad. I was just being my usual klutzy self."

Mom was examining my ankle. "It looks bad, Dick," she said to Dad. "We have to get her to that doctor Mrs. McConnell told us about."

"Come on, Tess," Dad said. "The car's right outside." He helped me to my feet—actually my foot—and as I leaned against him, I turned to Mrs. McConnell.

"Thanks again, Mrs. McConnell," I said. "If you hadn't come along, I'd probably still be sitting under that tree."

She smiled. "Just take care of yourself."

We were almost to the door, when I suddenly thought of something. "Mrs. McConnell, are those pictures on the table of your son?"

After a brief pause, she nodded. "Yes. That's my son Billy."

"That's a great picture of him and the dogs. He looks so happy. Does he live around here?" I asked.

A frozen look came over Mrs. McConnell's face. "Billy's dead," she said quietly. We all stared at her in appalled silence.

Mom managed to speak first. "I'm so sorry, Mrs. McConnell . . ."

I tried to think of something to say, but I couldn't find my voice.

"You better get along to the doctor now, Tess," Mrs. McConnell said gently.

I managed to mumble something and then hobbled outside, leaning against Dad. As we drove away, I looked back at the small white house, thinking of the photograph of the smiling boy who had once lived there.

Chapter Six

"How are you doing, Tess?" Mom asked, turning around from the front seat of Dad's car. I was sprawled in the back, my bad leg stretched out in front of me.

"I'm fine, Mom," I lied. Actually, I was feeling lousy. My ankle was throbbing, and worse than that, I couldn't stop thinking about Mrs. McConnell and her son. It was weird—I'd never met Billy McConnell and I hardly knew his mother, but I felt as if I had just heard that a friend or relative had died. Maybe it was seeing that picture of him as a kid, looking so happy.

Mom and Dad were quietly discussing something, and my attention tuned back in when I heard Dad say, "I hope she's right about this fellow Barry."

"Who, Dad?" I asked.

"Mrs. McConnell," Dad replied. "She told us to call a Dr. Barry in town—said he was the only one worth anything. I just caught him, too. He said he was about to go out the door."

I leaned back against the seat and sighed, feeling a sudden wave of homesickness for the comfortably old and familiar. I wanted to see my old house, my old friends, even my old doctor.

At last Dad pulled up in front of a building on Main Street. I could see a sign on the door that said "Jefferson Barry, M.D." *Jefferson?* I thought to myself, picturing an ancient southern gentleman with a white goatee.

Dad helped me out of the car and up to the door, with Mom trailing behind. The only person inside the doctor's office was a red-haired man who looked about Dad's age. He was wearing sweats and running shoes, and he smiled at us as we came in.

"This is the patient, I presume?" he asked. "Hi. I'm Jeff Barry."

That was a surprise! I'd been expecting Colonel Sanders, not this jovial jogger.

"Hello, Dr. Barry," Mom said. "We're the Lawrences, and this is our daughter, Tess."

"Well, Tess, let's have a look at that ankle," the doctor said. After Dad helped me into an examining room, he and Mom hovered near the door. "Why don't you folks go sit down in the waiting room?" Dr. Barry suggested. "This won't take long."

When Mom and Dad left, the doctor began examining my ankle. "I'm afraid you're out of the Boston Marathon," he joked as he gently prodded it. "Believe it or not, you're lucky. It's a bad sprain, but nothing appears to be broken."

"That's what Mrs. McConnell said," I told him.

"She did, did she? I'm glad she advised you to get a second opinion, anyway."

I smiled. "I guess she thinks you're a pretty good doctor."

"Mrs. Mac is one smart woman," Dr. Barry said, grinning. "Just to be on the safe side, though, I'm going to take an X ray in case she or I missed something."

"You know Mrs. McConnell pretty well, huh?"

The doctor nodded. "Sure do. I've known her since I was this high." He raised one hand about three feet from the floor. "I hung around the McConnells' all the time when I was a kid. My family lived just a ways down the road until we moved into town when I was in junior high."

"Then you must have known Mrs. McConnell's son Billy," I said.

Dr. Barry's smile faded slightly. "Yes, I knew Billy. He was a good friend of mine. As a matter of fact, I hear your injury is due to falling out of the tree house Billy and I built."

"You helped build it?" I asked, surprised.

He laughed. "Don't worry—I'm a much better doctor than a carpenter. It's a wonder Billy and I didn't break our necks on the thing. Of course, we were only about nine or ten at the time."

"Dr. Barry—" I hesitated. Part of me didn't want to find out what had happened to Billy McConnell, but curiosity won out. "How did Billy die?"

The doctor's smile vanished altogether. "He was killed in Vietnam." He sighed. "It was a

68

long time ago, but sometimes it seems like yesterday."

"That's terrible," I murmured.

I had imagined Billy dying in a car crash, like Luke's father, or of some awful illness, not getting killed in a war. Of course, I knew about Vietnam. Dad and Mom had been very active in the antiwar movement, and we had learned about it in school. But somehow it hadn't seemed real until now.

"Was Billy Mrs. McConnell's only child?" I asked.

Dr. Barry nodded. "She took his death pretty hard. And then her husband got sick and died just a few years later."

"Poor Mrs. McConnell," I said softly.

"I'm surprised that you know her," Dr. Barry said. "Mrs. Mac mostly keeps to herself."

"I met her when I climbed into the tree house for the first time. She was pretty mad at me, but then she got over it." I paused. "Dad says people call her Crazy Mary, but I don't see anything crazy about her."

Frowning, the doctor said, "People tend to think anyone who's different is crazy. Mrs. Mac's always been a strong-minded woman— a lot of people don't like that. Over the years she's had a few run-ins with folks around here. The last time was about five years ago when she had a couple of hunters arrested for trespassing on her land. It caused quite an uproar. In this town you don't sign complaints against hunters for trespassing. It just isn't done." He smiled. "But Mrs. Mac did it."

After taking an X ray of my ankle, Dr. Barry announced that I had nothing but a bad sprain. He wrapped the ankle with an elastic bandage and said I would have to stay off that foot for a few days. I hobbled out of the examining room on crutches.

"Better not try climbing any more trees for a while, Tess," he said as he saw Dad, Mom, and me to the door. "And if you happen to see Mrs. Mac, tell her I said hello."

I spent the rest of the weekend lounging around with my foot propped up, reading, watching TV, and thinking about Mrs. McConnell and Billy.

By Sunday evening my ankle was feeling a lot better, although I still couldn't put any weight on my left foot. The thought of going to school the next day on crutches wasn't very appealing, but the only alternative was staying home, and since I didn't want to be absent my second week at B.C. High, I decided to tough it out.

On Monday morning Mom dropped me off at a side entrance so I wouldn't have to hobble quite so far. I'd put my notebooks and textbooks in a backpack so my arms would be free to manipulate the crutches.

When Lenny saw me crutching past the office where she worked every morning before school, she ran outside into the hallway, exclaiming, "Tess, what happened?" When I told her my sad story, Lenny was torn between sympathy and amusement. She kept saying, "You fell out of a *tree house*? You've got to be kidding!"

As I clumsily made my way into chemistry class, I was dismayed to see several kids already there. Of course, they all wanted to know what had happened too.

"I just fell," I said nonchalantly, not wanting to go into the whole lengthy and ridiculous explanation again.

When I reached my lab table, I found Luke Stoddard sitting there. Before he could open his mouth, I said quickly, "I know what you're thinking, but no, I did *not* trip over my bag."

To my surprise, he grinned. "Well then, what *did* happen? An old football injury act up?"

A joke! Luke had actually made a joke! I laughed. "Believe it or not, it's even sillier than that," I began, sitting down and shoving my crutches under the table. I didn't have a chance to say more because Carter Davis arrived just then.

"Hey, Tess, what's this I hear about you being on crutches?" he asked.

"Okay," I said with a sigh, "I might as well confess. I fell out of a tree house."

"You did *what*?" Carter exclaimed.

"I don't know why everybody thinks that's so strange," I said huffily. "It could happen to anyone!"

Luke's grin broadened and Carter laughed out loud. "Gee, Tess, I didn't know you lived in a tree," Carter teased. "You'll have to invite me over sometime."

"It's not *my* tree house," I protested. "It's on my neighbor's property. I was exploring one day and I found it in this great big old tree. What can I say? I just had to climb it. . . ."

"Because it was there, like Mount Everest?" Luke put in.

Two jokes from Luke Stoddard in about two minutes! That had to be some sort of a record.

Grinning at him, I said, "You got it. I came, I climbed"—I paused dramatically—"and I fell! That's why I'm on crutches. It's just a sprain, so Dr. Barry said I'd have to use them for only a few days."

"So who's this neighbor with the tree house?" Carter asked. "If you ask me, it sounds like lawsuit time. You could make a bundle from this, Tess."

"No way!" I said emphatically. "It wasn't anybody's fault but mine that I climbed that tree like an idiot."

"Well, it sounds like a clear-cut case of negligence to me," Carter insisted. "Your parents should talk to a lawyer. You know, Tess, you could have killed yourself!"

"Too bad I didn't, huh?" I joked. "Then my parents could *really* clean up."

Carter didn't think it was funny. "Who is this neighbor, anyway?" he asked.

"Mrs. McConnell."

His eyes widened. "Crazy Mary? Wow! This is even better. Maybe you can have that old loony put away!"

I was getting ticked off. "She's not a loony, Carter. She's a very nice woman, and I like her."

"That's because you're new in town," Carter said loftily. "Folks around here know she has more than a few screws loose."

Now I was really mad. "Well, 'folks around here' are wrong! I think it's really rotten how unsympathetic people can be. Mrs. McConnell has had a very sad life. First her only son was killed in Vietnam, and then her husband got sick and died—"

"Chill out, Tess," Carter interrupted. "That was more than twenty-five years ago. She ought to be over it by now."

That did it! In my eyes, Carter Davis had just turned into a monumental creep. "For your information, there are some things a person *never* gets over!" I snapped.

Carter threw up his hands and cringed in mock fear. "Okay, okay! Don't get all riled up, Tess. You don't have to fly into a passion about it." He grinned suggestively. "But if you *do* get into a passion, why don't you get into one *with* me, not *at* me?"

"Oh, shut up, Carter!" I muttered. He just laughed, then strolled to the front of the room to talk to Mr. Todd, who had just come in.

Still fuming, I glanced over at Luke. He was giving me a very serious look. *I guess he thinks I'm really weird,* I thought. *Well, tough! I don't care.*

As I reached for my backpack and took out my chemistry notebook, Luke said, "Tess?"

I frowned. "What?"

"I just want you to know I'm on your side," he said softly. "I think it was great how you defended Mrs. McConnell."

When I met Luke's gaze, I saw genuine admiration in his blue eyes, and I felt myself blushing. "Thanks," I managed to say. "I just got so mad! When I think of everything Mrs. McConnell's been through—well, I just think people should be a little—I don't know—nicer, I guess."

"Most people aren't very nice," Luke said, and I was distressed by the bitterness in his voice. Suddenly he smiled at me. "I don't mean you. You're a very nice girl, Tess Lawrence."

I wasn't sure how to react. Usually when a guy says a girl is "nice," he means she's boring, or a goody-goody. Guys don't seem to put "nice" at the top of their list of requirements for girls. But the way Luke said it made me feel as if I'd been given the best compliment of my entire life.

"Thanks," I said again, smiling back at him. Then I added, "And now I'm going to give you a chance to prove how nice *you* can be, Luke Stoddard."

He raised his eyebrows. "How?"

"By letting you show me what answer you got for problem seven in our chemistry homework. It has me stumped."

Laughing, he opened his notebook and began explaining the problem to me.

Chapter Seven

The rest of the week I was continually amazed by the change that had come over Luke. He was actually friendly, asking me how my ankle was coming along and talking about the various classes we had together. It wasn't as if he suddenly started gabbing his head off or anything like that. Luke was still pretty quiet most of the time, but since up until then I was used to hearing two or three words max from him, it was pretty astonishing.

The rare Stoddard smile appeared a lot more frequently too, and he even made a few more really funny jokes, delivered deadpan in that southern drawl of his. One day Luke whispered a joke to me during English class and I almost turned blue trying not to laugh out loud.

After class, as Lenny and I were walking down the hall, she asked, "What was so funny, Tess? I thought you were going to fall on the floor any minute."

I laughed. "Oh, Luke just made this crack and it broke me up. Ms. Wallace gave me such a dirty look! I could have killed him."

Carter Davis was walking behind us and butted into our conversation. "I never knew Stoddard was such a comedian," he said sarcastically.

I didn't reply. I was still very angry at Carter for calling Mrs. McConnell a loony. I guess he wasn't used to getting the deep-freeze treatment from a female, because he turned red and stalked off down the corridor.

When the second week of school ended, I felt that I was starting to fit in at last. Memories of my old life seemed to be fading a bit, and it wasn't nearly so painful when I got calls or letters from Melissa and my other friends from Glen Forest.

I know Mom and Dad were relieved that I was adjusting so well, and so was I. I guess that was because I had made a lot of new friends. They were really great kids, Lenny especially, and not all that different from the kids at Glen Forest High—a little less sophisticated, maybe, but that was fine with me. On Saturday I had Lenny and some of the girls over. We had a great time gossiping, giggling, and listening to CDs.

On Sunday afternoon I did my homework for a while and then took my guitar out to the porch. I was all by myself because Mom and Dad were playing golf at the country club with Carter's parents. They were getting pretty chummy with Judge Davis and his wife, which didn't exactly thrill me, since I wasn't so keen on Carter at the moment. As for Carly, she continued to give me dirty looks in chorus, so I kept out of her way as much as possible.

I sat in the porch swing, enjoying the warm, sunny September afternoon and belting out some of my favorite rock songs. Then, for a change of pace, I started picking out the chords to "Danny Boy." Ever since we had sung it in chorus I had become really fond of the song and had made an effort to learn it. "Danny Boy" never failed to move me deeply as I imagined the pain of a mother seeing a son off to war. Of course, every time I sang it now, I thought of Mrs. McConnell and her son who never came back. It made the song all the more poignant to me.

I sang the last verse softly, almost pleadingly:

> Then come ye back, when summer's in
> the meadow,
> Or when the valley's hushed and white
> with snow.
> Then I'll be there, in sunshine or in
> shadow.
> Oh, Danny boy, oh, Danny boy, I love
> you so.

As the last note died away, I sat in silence for a minute, cradling my guitar in my arms and still thinking of Billy. When I looked up, I was surprised to see Mrs. McConnell standing by the porch steps, holding a large paper bag. I jumped up from the swing and smiled, walking over toward her.

"Hi, Mrs. McConnell—" I broke off, distressed to see a tear rolling down her cheek. "Mrs. McConnell? Are you okay?"

She quickly wiped the tear away with one

hand. "Yes, I'm all right. It's such a lovely song and you sing it so beautifully, Tess."

"Thanks," I said. "Why don't you come up and sit on the porch with me for a while?"

She made her way up the steps and sat down on the swing, putting the bag down on the floor by her feet. I sat down next to her.

"I was wondering how y'all were getting along with your ankle," she said.

"Oh, I'm fine," I assured her. "You were right—it was just a bad sprain. I had to use crutches for a couple of days, but now I'm pretty much back to normal."

"That's good," she said. Indicating the bag, she added, "I brought your family some apples and some jam I made. There's some peach and some quince."

"Quince?" I must have sounded a little skeptical, because she smiled.

"You've never had quince jam?" she asked.

I shook my head. "I've never even heard of it. What's a quince?"

"It's a fruit," Mrs. McConnell explained. "It's big and yellow and sort of fuzzy-skinned. You can't eat it raw because it's sour as anything, but it's real good in jam."

I made a face, and this time she laughed.

"That's how my Billy used to look at me when he was little and I told him that beets was really good and that he should at least try them."

"And did he?"

She nodded. "Yep, and he hated 'em!"

Grinning, I said, "I'm with Billy on that one. But I'm sure the quince jam is great. Thanks, Mrs. McConnell."

"You're more than welcome." Then she looked down at my guitar. "You sure are good on that thing, Tess. I always wished I could play an instrument like that. And you sing so pretty. I sing like a crow myself."

I laughed. "C'mon, Mrs. McConnell. Like a crow?"

"No, come to think of it, a crow sounds bet-ter'n me." I laughed again and Mrs. McConnell stood up. "Well, I reckon I better get back. I just wanted to check up on you. Did you like Jeff Barry all right?"

"Yeah, he was great," I said. "He told me to tell you hello for him." I hesitated, then blurted out, "Mrs. McConnell, I never said how sorry I am about your son. Dr. Barry told me about him. I mean, about him getting killed in Viet-nam and all ..." I stopped awkwardly. "I'm—I'm really sorry," I stammered.

She sat down again on the swing and sighed. "Thank you, Tess. Billy wasn't much older than you when he enlisted. It was ridiculous, my Billy supposed to be killing people! He couldn't even stand to kill one of our chickens. I can't stand to kill any of them now, either. But Billy went over there. He wrote me letters, trying to act like things wasn't so bad, but I could tell they was."

She was silent for a couple of minutes and then spoke again. "You know, that first day I met you, you gave me quite a start, being up in Billy's old tree house. And then you said something about being homesick for a tree. You see, in one of Billy's letters he was telling me about all the different types of trees in Vietnam. He said, 'Ma, they're really beautiful, but boy, am I homesick for our old Kentucky trees.' "

"I wish I had known him, Mrs. McConnell," I murmured.

She smiled sadly at me. "I wish you had too, Tess." She got up again. "Now I really am going. Take care of yourself, you hear?"

I nodded. Mrs. McConnell left the porch and headed toward the back of our yard. I sat on the porch for a long time after she had gone, just gazing off at the distant trees and wondering which ones Billy had missed most.

September seemed to rush by in no time. Almost before I knew it, it was the second week of October. The weather was still warm, but the nights were getting a bit nippy and the trees were starting to dress in their fall shades of yellow, orange, and red.

School was going along all right. I'd already had several tests and handed in a few papers. In chemistry we had done a couple of experiments and somehow managed not to blow up the place. I enjoyed chem lab because it gave me a chance to talk to Luke. He was finally opening up a lot more, although certain subjects still seemed to be taboo.

One of the forbidden topics was his family. Luke also steered clear of any talk about his being a musician. I tried a couple of times to ask him about it, but he always changed the subject. So I took the hint, even though I was awfully curious about The Stompin' Stoddards.

In chorus Mr. Cassin was beginning to talk about our Christmas concert and the spring musical. I couldn't help wondering how in the world you could put on any kind of a musical with only twenty people, especially when only two of them were guys. It promised to be pretty interesting.

Then on Friday at chorus practice, Mr. Cassin announced a countywide talent show. He said there was going to be a big prize for the winner—$2,500 in college scholarship money. When he explained that somebody named Tommy Lee Redmond had donated the prize, the entire chorus got all excited. They were even more thrilled when Mr. Cassin said that Tommy Lee would be one of the judges.

Turning to Lenny, I whispered, "Who the heck is Tommy Lee Redmond?"

She stared at me in astonishment. "You don't know who *Tommy Lee Redmond* is? Why, he's B.C.'s most famous son!"

"Never heard of him," I confessed. "So who is he? The local Donald Trump or something?"

Lenny giggled. "You've got to be kidding, Tess! Tommy Lee is making a really big name for himself in country and western music. You know his song 'Truck-Drivin' Woman,' don't you?"

"Gee," I said dryly, "I guess I must have missed that one somehow."

"Well, it was way up there on the C & W

charts last year. Tommy Lee's going to be a really big star someday, just you wait and see."

"I guess I will," I said. "Anyway, it's nice of him to give money for a scholarship." We had to end our conversation there because Mr. Cassin was giving us the eye.

After chorus Lenny walked with me to my locker. "You're going to enter the talent show, aren't you, Tess?" she asked eagerly.

"I don't know. . . ."

"You've just got to," Lenny announced. "Otherwise Carly Davis will be sure to win. Of course, she might win anyway just because she's a Davis. But it sure would be nice for her to have some competition for a change."

Before I could reply, Carly's brother came over to us. "Hi, girls," Carter said with one of those dazzling smiles.

I smiled back at him. Carter had made a major effort to get on my good side again, and I had finally given in. I mean, I don't believe in holding grudges, especially against someone who could be as charming as Carter Davis.

Lenny had told me that Carter had broken up with Diana Webber that week. She'd also warned me that he was preparing to pounce on me any minute now. When I just shrugged, Lenny had frowned at me. "Don't tell me you actually *want* to go out with him?" she asked.

"I guess there could be worse fates," I replied casually.

Lenny's frown deepened. "Yeah, like dating King Kong!"

Now, as Carter stood with us at our lockers, she eyed him disapprovingly. She suddenly looked over at me and said, "Listen, I've got to go, Tess. See you later." Pointedly ignoring Carter, she hurried off.

"Alone at last, Tess." He smiled at me and there was a look in those beautiful hazel eyes of his that made me wonder if maybe Lenny was right. He almost looked like a lion ready to pounce on its unsuspecting prey—me.

I turned back to my locker and fished out some books. "Gee, Carter, I've really got to rush," I said, "or I'll miss my bus."

"Your bus?" Carter repeated with disdain. "A girl like you shouldn't have to ride the bus. What's wrong with your old man? Why doesn't he buy you a car?"

Although I had been trying to talk Dad into getting me a car for some time, I was slightly resentful of Carter's criticism. "He doesn't want to spoil me," I said coolly, trying to close my temperamental locker.

Carter slammed one large hand against it and it clicked shut. "Well, *I'd* sure like to spoil you," he purred, moving a little closer.

"Terrific, Carter," I said, pretending to take him seriously. "In that case, I'd like a baby-blue Jaguar." He threw back his head and laughed. "But until you give me one," I said, "I've got to catch that bus."

"Forget the bus," Carter said. "I'll give you a ride home."

"But it's out of your way . . ." I began.

"Hey, who cares about a few extra miles? C'mon, you've never ridden my wheels before." He said this as if it were an opportunity that no girl in her right mind could possibly pass up, so I finally agreed.

When we reached the parking lot, Carter stopped next to a gleaming forest-green convertible and gallantly opened the door for me. As I got inside, I was definitely impressed by the plush interior. "Great car, Carter," I said, fastening my seat belt.

He just smiled. A moment later he got in, popped a cassette into the tape deck, and we were on our way. It was a summery day, so Carter had the top down. My hair whipped around my face as we sped down the highway.

As we drove along, Carter began talking about football. Or I guess I should say he began shouting so I could hear him over the noise of rock music blasting from the car speakers, not to mention the wind. Since Carter was one of B.C. High's star football players, it was a subject near and dear to his heart. I'm not a football fan—most of the time I don't even know what's going on during a game—so the subject wasn't particularly fascinating to me. But I nodded politely as Carter gave me his opinion of the different teams in the conference.

We were nearing the road where we would turn off to go to my house, when I suddenly spied a vehicle pulled off on the shoulder. As we got closer, I recognized Luke Stoddard's old pickup truck. The hood was up and someone was peering under it.

"It looks as if Luke's having some trouble with his truck," I said to Carter.

Carter grinned. "It's not surprising, with that rust bucket." To my consternation, he barely slowed down as he drove by the disabled truck.

"Hey, Stoddard!" he shouted. "Get a horse!" Luke looked up as we whizzed past, and I could see the look of anger on his face.

"That was really juvenile, Carter," I said in disgust. "Did you ever think about stopping to see if he needed help?"

"Help Stoddard?" Carter said incredulously. "No way. He's a grease monkey—he has to be with that pathetic thing he drives. He doesn't need any help."

"Well, it would've been a nice gesture," I snapped.

Carter glanced at me in surprise. "What is it with you and Stoddard, anyway?" he asked.

"What do you mean?"

"I mean, you seem awfully interested in the guy. How come?"

"I happen to like Luke," I said. "He's a nice person."

"Yeah, right—nice," Carter sneered. "I can't figure out why you'd even give him the time of day, Tess. The Stoddards are low-life. Haven't you heard that Luke's old man was the county's biggest lush?"

By this point my hands were clenched into fists and I had to make a huge effort to control my temper. "Not everyone can have a wealthy judge for a father!" I said.

Carter snorted. "Meet Tess Lawrence, defender of the poor and downtrodden!"

"Well, it's better than being the defender of the rich and obnoxious!" I shot back. Carter just scowled.

We drove the rest of the way to my house in total silence. The minute he stopped the car, I quickly got out. "Thanks a lot, Carter," I said sarcastically, slamming the door and hurrying into the house.

"What a jerk!" I muttered as I threw my books down on the table in the hall. "Serves me right for not listening to Lenny." I glanced out the window and saw Carter gun his car down the gravel driveway on his way back to the road.

I went up to my room, and as I changed my clothes, I suddenly had the urge to see if Luke was still on the highway, working on his truck. But then, remembering the expression on his face as Carter and I drove by, I decided against it. Somehow I figured he wouldn't be very pleased to see me.

That night I had a hard time getting to sleep.

I kept thinking about Luke, and hearing Carter say "The Stoddards are low-life." The more I thought about it, the madder I got.

I woke up the next morning determined to prove to Luke that I wasn't in the same creepy league with Carter Davis. After lunch I persuaded Mom to let me drive her car to the store, casually offering to fill up the tank with gas while I was in town. I wasn't even sure that Luke would be working at the gas station that afternoon, but I felt it was worth a shot.

As I pulled up to the station, there was no sign of him, and I felt a jab of disappointment. Another gas station attendant was busy helping a little old lady in a monster Buick, so I got out of Mom's car and somewhat halfheartedly took the pump handle in one hand while I tried to move the lever on the pump with the other. It wouldn't budge. I struggled for a couple of minutes until I heard someone come up behind me.

When I turned around, I saw that the person was Luke. All of a sudden I felt really nervous. I'm sure I sounded like an idiot when I said, "Uh—hi, Luke. Gee, it looks like déjà vu all over again, huh?"

He just gave me a cold, unfriendly look. I

babbled on. "The day my family moved here we came to this gas station and the pump lever was stuck then too. Do you remember?"

"Yeah, I remember." Luke leaned over to the pump, banged the lever into position, and then started to leave.

"Luke, wait a minute," I cried.

He stopped and glared at me. "What?"

"I just wanted to tell you I'm sorry that Carter didn't stop yesterday when you were having trouble with your truck. He can be a real pain sometimes."

"Yeah, but he's a good-looking, well-heeled pain, right?" Luke muttered.

I scowled at him. "What's your problem, anyway?"

"Hey, no problem," he said with a shrug. "What do I care if you go out with that fathead Davis? Like they say, birds of a feather."

Now I was getting ticked off. "What exactly do you mean by that? Are you saying I'm a fathead like Carter?"

"No, that's not what I meant," Luke replied. "But the two of you belong to the same club."

"Club? What club?"

"Oh, c'mon, you know what I mean. The money club. The my-family-is-hot-stuff club.

Yeah, I remember that first day you came here. 'This town is a total Hicksville,' you said. Well, now you have good old Carter to make up for it."

Really furious, I shoved the gas pump hose into his hands. "Here!" I shouted. "Keep your stupid gas!"

Then I got back into Mom's car and literally burned rubber as I shot out of the station lot. Glancing in the rearview mirror, I had one last glimpse of Luke standing there, staring after me, still holding the gas pump hose.

Chapter Eight

To say I wasn't looking forward to school on Monday morning would be an understatement. I was not eager to see either Carter or Luke, and as I walked slowly down the hall toward chemistry, I vowed that I would just ignore them both.

It wasn't easy, however, because Carter was already sitting at his lab table when I came into the lab. I gave him an icy look as I stalked past him to my own table and sat down. He immediately turned around and smiled at me.

"You're not still mad at me, are you, Tess?" he asked. When I didn't say anything, his smile vanished. "C'mon, Tess, give me a break, okay? I was just joking around about Stoddard and his truck."

"I didn't think it was very funny," I said stiffly.

Raising his right hand, Carter said solemnly, "I promise I won't do it again, no matter what. The next time Stoddard's old bucket of bolts breaks down, I'll tow it to the garage myself. Heck, I'll *push it* to the garage myself."

"Yeah, right," I said. I tried not to smile, but the picture of Carter pushing Luke's pickup down the highway was too ridiculous and I couldn't help it.

Carter beamed. "That's more like it!" He was ready to say something else, but just then Brad came along and started talking to him.

As the rest of the kids came in, I kept waiting for Luke to show up, but there was no sign of him. The final bell rang and there was still no Luke. When Mr. Todd began his lecture, I found it hard to concentrate on chemistry because I kept wondering why Luke was absent.

The next day the same thing happened. No Luke. When he still wasn't in school on Wednesday, I started worrying that he was really sick, or that something serious had happened to him.

It seemed like an unusually long day, and as I walked down the stairs after chorus, I was glad to be going home. I felt depressed for some reason, and for the first time in a while I wished that I'd never moved to Blossom Creek.

I ran into Mr. Todd at the bottom of the stairs. He smiled at me and I managed to smile back.

"Miss Lawrence, do you happen to know what's wrong with that lab partner of yours?" he asked.

I shrugged. "No, I don't. I guess he must have a bad cold or something."

"Hmmm . . ." Mr. Todd shook his head. "Maybe you could give him a call, Tess. Find out when he's coming back. He'd probably appreciate having someone to help him catch up on things. You're also in some of Luke's other classes, aren't you?"

"Yes," I said, trying to sound casual. "I guess I could call him. . . ."

"Good!" said Mr. Todd. "That would be real neighborly of you. Well, I've got to get to wrestling practice before the boys start tying each other in knots. A coach's work is never done."

We said good-bye, and I went outside to wait for the bus. Had I actually said I would call Luke? Remembering our last encounter at the gas station, I very much doubted if he would be pleased at getting a "neighborly" call from me.

When I got home, I quickly thumbed through the phone book and found a listing under "Stoddard, Charles." Since I'd heard that Luke's father's name was Charlie, I figured that must be his house. I took a deep breath, then picked up the phone and dialed.

I waited nervously while the phone rang at the other end. A boy whose voice I didn't recognize finally answered it and said Luke wasn't home. When I asked when he would be back, there was a long pause. "I don't know," said the kid on the other end. He sounded wary. "I'm Jason, Luke's brother. Can I take a message?"

"Well . . ." I hesitated. "This is Tess Lawrence. Luke and I are in some of the same classes, and—well, I thought—I mean, he's been out all week and I just wondered when he was coming back to school. He's missed a lot, and I thought maybe I could go over our homework assignments with him. Unless he's coming back tomorrow, of course."

"No, he'll be out again, Tess," Jason said. He suddenly sounded a lot more friendly. "But I bet Luke would like it if you'd come over and help him out with his homework."

To my surprise, I found myself agreeing to stop by the Stoddard house the next afternoon after school. After getting directions from Jason, I hung up the phone, wondering what I had gotten myself into. I could just imagine Luke's reaction when Jason told him some girl named Tess was going to drop off his homework after school tomorrow. *Oh, well,* I thought, *no big deal. I'm just doing this because Mr. Todd suggested it. It's nothing personal, nothing at all.*

Mom let me borrow her car the next day, and as soon as school was out I headed for Luke's house. Turning onto Peach Street, I slowed down to read the numbers. When I found 503, I came to a stop in front of a large, somewhat run-down–looking two-story frame house. This must be the place, I thought uncomfortably as I turned off the ignition and gathered up my notebooks.

There was a small bicycle on the front walk with what looked like a dog-chewed Frisbee next to it. I climbed up the steps and crossed the porch, pausing when I reached the partly open front door. I could hear fiddle music coming from inside, and as I listened I realized that the fiddler must be Luke. It was a lively tune and I marveled at how well he played it. Then I remembered Lenny saying that Luke's father had been one of the best fiddle players in Kentucky and Luke was even better than his father.

When the music stopped I hesitated a moment more, then knocked on the door. A dog started barking somewhere inside. I heard footsteps coming toward me, and then the door swung all the way open. Luke stood there, a look of utter astonishment on his face. He was wearing a pair of ragged jeans and a plaid shirt over a white T-shirt, and he looked weary and disheveled. His dark hair was touseled and he needed a shave.

"Tess? What're you doing here?" he asked. It was immediately obvious that my visit was totally unexpected.

"Hi, Luke," I said somewhat sheepishly. "Didn't your brother tell you I was going to drop by?"

"Which brother?" Before I could reply, he said, "Let me guess. My brother Jason, right?" I nodded and Luke frowned. "That bonehead! No, he didn't tell me, and I'm going to wring his neck."

He sure wasn't making me feel very welcome. "Oh, well, it's no big deal," I said in embarrassment. "I told Jason I'd bring over the homework assignments you missed, but if you're busy . . ."

I started to turn away, but to my surprise Luke quickly stepped out onto the porch and touched my arm.

"I didn't mean for you to go, Tess," he said. "I'm just irked at my brother for not—"

"Warning you?" I finished for him.

Luke smiled. "Telling me," he corrected me.

"Well, Mr. Todd suggested that you might want to find out what homework we've had, since you've been out all week," I told him.

"Oh, I already got the assignments," Luke said. "But thanks, anyway, Tess. It was real nice of you to go to this trouble and all."

"Oh, that's okay," I said. "I guess I'd better get going, then."

"What's your hurry?" Luke asked. "Can't you

stick around a few minutes?" When I didn't answer immediately, he quickly continued. "Listen, Tess, I'm sorry about Saturday. I didn't
have any right to talk to you the way I did.
Just because I don't happen to like Carter—
well, anyway, I'm sorry."

He looked so genuinely contrite that I smiled.
"Don't worry about it," I said. "Let's forget it,
okay?" Then I added, "I heard you playing just
now. You're really good."

A faint flush appeared on his face. "Thanks,"
he mumbled, running a hand through his hair.

"Gosh, I didn't even ask you how you're feeling," I said. "I hope you're better."

"Oh, I wasn't sick," Luke said.

"You weren't?"

"No. My little sister got sick and Mom
couldn't take off work. She just started this
new job."

"That's too bad," I said. "About your sister
being sick and you having to miss school to
take care of her, I mean."

Luke shrugged. "Oh, I don't think I missed
all that much. My aunt Betty has the day off
tomorrow, so she's going to be able to stay
with Annie."

Just then a pathetic voice wailed, "Luke!" He

grinned. "That's my patient. Want to come in for a minute and say hello?"

"Well, okay," I said. "But just for a minute."

I started to follow Luke inside. Suddenly he turned and said, "Whoa! I forgot to ask—have you ever had chicken pox?"

"Yes, Dr. Stoddard. I had it when I was four and a half and I was thoroughly miserable."

"Good," he said, and then laughed. "I mean, it's good you've already had it, not that you were miserable. C'mon in." This time we both went into the house and were immediately met by a small, scruffy-looking dog who barked frantically at me.

"That's Fluff," Luke said. "Don't mind her. Her bark is much worse than her bite."

I leaned over and petted the dog. "Hi, Fluff," I said, scratching her behind the ears. "How you doing?"

"*Luke!*" came the child's voice again.

"Coming," Luke called out. "Guess what, Annie? We've got company."

He led the way into the kitchen with Fluff trotting at his heels. A small, dark-haired girl in red pajamas sat at the kitchen table. What I assumed was Luke's fiddle lay on the table next to a stack of paper and a pile of crayons.

The little girl eyed me curiously as I came in. She looked about five or six years old, and she would have been pretty except for the sprinkling of scabby pink spots on her face.

"Annie, this is Tess," Luke said.

"Hi, Tess." The child smiled, then sighed tragically. "I have chicken pox!"

I came over and sat down at the table next to her. "I know. Your brother told me. It's not much fun, is it?"

"It sure isn't," Annie agreed. "The spots are all itchy now, but Luke said I mustn't scratch them."

"He's right about that," I said. "I remember when I had the chicken pox a long time ago. My grandma was taking care of me and she said if I scratched them, I'd get the chicken's curse on me."

Annie's eyes widened. "What's that?"

"Grandma said I would turn into a chicken!"

Annie giggled. "Your grandma sounds silly," she said.

"Yeah, she's real silly," I said, grinning. "That's one of the reasons I like her."

Luke leaned back against the kitchen counter. "Why don't you show Tess your picture, Annie?"

The little girl picked up the piece of paper in front of her. It was a brilliantly colored drawing of a horse with a gigantic smiling sun behind it.

"Oh, that's really good," I said. "I guess you must like horses, huh?" She nodded. "I've always liked horses too."

"My daddy said he would get me a horse one day—" Annie began, then stopped and started picking through the crayons. "Purple's my favorite color," she said abruptly. "What's yours?"

"Blue, I guess," I said.

From Annie's expression, I gathered that in her opinion this was a very poor choice. She put a blank piece of paper in front of me. "You want to draw something?"

"Well, okay," I said. "What should I draw?"

Annie thought about it for a moment, then pointed at her brother. "Draw Luke."

"Hmm," I said, meeting Luke's amused gaze, "I'm not very good at portraits. Maybe I'd better do an abstract picture of him."

"A what?" asked Annie with a puzzled look.

"An abstract picture. That's a picture that doesn't really look like what it's supposed to be. Here, I'll show you." I drew a big circle, put a few lines through it and a triangle on top. "There! I call it 'Luke in the Kitchen'!"

Annie looked at it and grinned. "It does too look like him." She giggled.

Luke walked over to the table and glanced down at my picture. "Thanks a bunch, Tess," he said with a wry grin. "You really think my head's that pointed, huh?"

Annie was so delighted by his comment that she giggled even harder.

When she had finally sobered up, I said, "Well, now that we've displayed our artistic talents, Annie, maybe your brother would show us one of his." I turned to Luke. "Would you play a song for us?"

"Yeah, Luke," Annie said eagerly. "Play 'Gray Eagle' again."

Luke was reluctant at first, but we browbeat him until he finally gave in. He picked up the fiddle and began playing the same lively song I had heard while I was standing on the front porch. When he finished, both Annie and I clapped.

"That was terrific!" I said.

"Now play the bear song," Annie ordered.

"I don't think so . . ." Luke began.

"Please, please, please?" Annie begged.

"Please, please, please?" I echoed.

Luke grinned and shook his head. "Okay, okay, I'll do it. But I need my guitar for that."

"You play the guitar too?" I asked.

"And the harmonica," Annie told me proudly. "I only play the guitar a little. Luke's teaching me."

"That's great," I said.

Luke had gone out of the room and now he returned with a guitar. "Okay, you asked for it. The bear song."

He struck a chord, then started playing and singing in a deep, mellow voice about Uncle Walter, who used to go waltzing with bears. It was such a silly song that I laughed as hard as Annie did. After a couple of verses he stopped and said, "Now you guys join in on the refrain, okay?"

We nodded and laughingly sang along with him. When the song ended, Luke smiled at me. "Hey, I didn't know you sang, Tess."

I shrugged. "Doesn't everybody?"

"Yeah, but I mean, you really *sing*. You're good, I mean it."

"Tess, now you have to sing a song all by yourself," commanded Annie.

"Oh, I don't know . . ." I murmured, feeling suddenly shy.

"Please, please, please?" said Luke.

Laughing, I said, "All right, you win. Let's see—what should I sing?"

"How about something a little more serious?" said Luke. "I'm worn out from all this giggling." That made Annie giggle again.

"Well," I said, "I guess I could sing a song I learned in French class last year. It's a lullaby."

"Good!" Annie chirped. "Maybe it'll put Luke to sleep."

"Now, Miss Annie, show some respect for your elders," Luke said with mock severity. Turning to me, he added, "The only problem is I don't know any French lullabies. Can you sing it unaccompanied?"

"I could, but if you don't mind, I'd rather play your guitar."

Luke smiled and handed it over. "Be my guest."

I just love French. Sometimes, I wish I *were* French so I could speak it all the time. As I sang the lullaby, I met Luke's eyes. He was watching me so intently that I faltered and almost forgot the lyrics for a moment. Somehow I managed to get through the song, and when it was over, Annie said, "You really sing pretty, Tess. Doesn't she sing pretty, Luke?"

Luke smiled at her and then at me. "She sings like an angel," he said softly. "A French angel."

I blushed. Suddenly my heart started racing. Until then, I had refused to admit to myself that I was falling in love with Luke Stoddard, but when he said that and smiled at me, I knew I was past all hope. I just wanted to get out of there as fast as possible before I gave myself away.

"I—I guess I really should be going," I said, putting down the guitar. "It was nice meeting you, Annie. I hope you get over your chicken pox real soon."

As I started toward the door, I heard Annie whisper loudly to Luke, "I really like Tess. Is she your girlfriend?"

Luke mumbled something to her that I couldn't hear, then followed me into the living room.

"You really have a wonderful voice, Tess," he said, gazing deeply into my eyes. He might have said something more, but Fluff suddenly began barking wildly. I heard a loud commotion outside, and four rowdy boys who seemed to range in age from about eight to thirteen stampeded through the front door. When they saw Luke and me, they stopped dead and stared at us.

Luke looked at me with a wry expression. "The horde returning from a day at school. These are my brothers, Tess. Davey, Sam, Jim, and"—he scowled at the oldest boy—"Jason. Guys, this is Tess."

Jason groaned and slapped his hand against his forehead. "Oh, jeez, Luke, I forgot to tell you she was coming over!" Then he grinned. "But it was no big deal, right? I mean, you were just hanging around anyway, weren't you?"

"Jace . . ." Luke said in a threatening tone, but Jason ignored him and turned to me.

"Hi, Tess. Sorry I forgot to give Luke your message, but I bet he was glad to see you."

"Well," I said, smiling, "at least he was surprised."

Luke was still frowning at Jason. "Tess has to go home now," he said. "Jason, you can go start dinner."

His younger brother sighed. "Okay, slave-driver." Then he grinned at me. "Well, bye, Tess. Come again real soon."

Luke walked outside with me. When we reached Mom's car, he said, "I don't think Jace forgot at all. He's a great one for jokes." He paused. "Thanks again for coming, Tess. You cheered Annie up a lot."

"Oh, I enjoyed it, especially the sing-along part." Getting into the car, I said, "Well, I guess I'll see you in school tomorrow."

Luke smiled. "You sure will."

I turned the key in the ignition, and as I pulled away from the curb, I looked back at him and waved. Luke waved back. All the way home I found myself humming the song about Uncle Walter waltzing with bears.

Chapter Nine

I was still in a good mood the next day as I stood in front of my locker, taking out my notebooks for my morning classes. I was debating whether or not I needed to lug along my chemistry textbook, when to my delight Luke appeared beside me.

I smiled happily at him. "Hi!" I said. "Welcome back. How's Annie?"

"Oh, she's much better. Mom thinks she'll be able to go back to school on Monday."

"That's good," I said. "She's really a cute kid."

There was a brief pause before Luke spoke

again. "Tess," he said hesitantly, "I was wondering—" He broke off.

"Wondering what?"

"Well, I was just thinking. Are you going to enter that talent show, the one Tommy Lee Redmond is sponsoring?"

"The talent show?" I said, somewhat surprised. "Gee, I'd forgotten all about it. I don't know if I'm brave enough. I mean, I just started school here and—"

"You really should, Tess. Like I told you yesterday, you're really good."

I blushed. "Thanks. Are *you* going to be in it? You're really good too."

Luke grinned. "Seems like the votes are in. We're both good. That's why I thought—" He paused again and then finished hurriedly, "I thought maybe we could do a number together."

I stared at him. "Do a number together?" I repeated stupidly. "You and me?"

"Yeah," he said, "I think we'd have a good chance of winning and we could split the prize money."

"Oh, Luke," I said, feeling a little stunned. "I don't know . . ."

"Hey, that's okay," he said quickly. "I don't

want to pressure you or anything. If you don't want to, I'll understand."

"Wait a minute!" I exclaimed. "I didn't say I wouldn't do it. You just took me by surprise, that's all. I mean, why don't you just enter by yourself? Then if you won, you'd get all the money."

Luke shook his head. "I don't think I'd have half as good a chance going solo," he said. "Ever since I heard you sing yesterday, I've been thinking about it, and I figured that the two of us would be a sure thing."

I laughed. "You're kidding! A sure thing?"

"Yeah, why not?" He smiled at me. "Besides, I thought it might be kind of fun playing together too."

I was so thrilled that Luke actually wanted me to sing with him that I said impulsively, "Okay, I'll do it! But what'll we sing? I've never really been into country music, and since Tommy Lee is one of the judges, I doubt he'll appreciate rock or show tunes."

"You're right there," Luke agreed. "But, heck, you'd be great doing country, Tess. I thought maybe we could do a country ballad. In fact, I've been working on one that might be just right for us."

"You write songs too?" I asked, impressed. Luke Stoddard certainly was full of surprises, not to mention talent!

"Yeah, I've written a few," he said casually. "Some of them aren't all that good, but I think this one is pretty decent. I'd like to see what *you* think."

That made me a little nervous. What if I thought Luke's song was awful? But I just said, "I can't wait to hear it. I bet it's terrific. I'll sign us up with Mr. Cassin today. We don't have a whole lot of time—the contest is less than a month away."

"Yeah, I know. I thought maybe we could get together this weekend and start rehearsing."

"Sounds good," I said, hoping I didn't sound as excited as I felt. Good? It sounded wonderful, marvelous, fabulous!

"What about tomorrow afternoon?" Luke suggested.

"Great! Want to come over to my house around two o'clock?"

Luke nodded. "Sure. But you'll have to tell me where you live."

I told him, and we discussed our practice session as we walked together to chemistry.

*   *   *

The next morning I casually informed Mom and Dad about the talent show and that I was going to enter it with Luke Stoddard, a guy I'd met at school. I also mentioned, almost as an afterthought, that Luke was coming over to our house that afternoon so we could rehearse.

Well, of course my nonchalance didn't work. Mom and Dad were instantly on the alert and began the usual parental inquisition. They wanted to know exactly who Luke Stoddard was and my casual answer, "Oh, just a guy in my class," didn't satisfy them at all. Parents can be pretty ridiculous sometimes. Every time you talk about a new guy, they always act as if you're going to take up with some Hell's Angel or something.

After a while they let up on me. I guess they figured since Luke was coming to the house, they would get a chance to grill him themselves. I just hoped they wouldn't embarrass me to death!

Following my news about Luke, Mom informed me that we were having company for dinner that night. I was far from pleased when I found out that the company was Judge Davis and his family.

"The whole family is coming?" I asked in dismay.

"That's the idea," Dad said. "Actually, the judge isn't sure if his kids could make it, being Saturday night and all, but your mother invited them."

"Myra Davis tells me her son Carter is in your class," Mom added.

"Yeah, he's in my class," I said unenthusiastically. "And his sister Carly's in chorus."

"I hear Carter's quite a football player," Dad said.

I groaned inwardly. Dad was a football nut, and I could foresee an entire evening discussing B.C. High's team and the Chicago Bears. But then I decided to look on the bright side. As Dad had said, it was Saturday night, and both Carter and Carly probably had dates.

After lunch, as I waited for Luke, I found myself getting increasingly nervous. If his song was really dreadful, what was I going to do? What if our voices didn't blend well? What if the entire thing was a disaster and Luke went back to being his old, unapproachable self?

At almost precisely two o'clock, Luke's old pickup truck pulled up into the drive. Dad looked out the window. "Is that your musician friend, Tess, driving that heap?" he asked.

"That's him," I said, hurrying to the front door.

Luke came up on the porch, toting his guitar case. "Hi, Tess," he said as I let him in.

As he stepped inside, he looked around and gave a low whistle. "Nice house," he said. Then I led him into the living room to get the parental scrutiny over with as soon as possible. Fortunately, Mom and Dad behaved themselves and soon left to drive into town.

I went upstairs and got my guitar. When I came down, I found Luke looking at some photographs of me in a frame on the living room wall. It was one of those frames that have spots for various pictures and Mom had filled them with photos of me from babyhood to the present.

Luke grinned at me and I shook my head. "I know. It's sort of embarrassing, but what can I do? At least my folks didn't have my baby shoes bronzed and on display."

He studied the pictures again. "I guess you don't have any brothers or sisters, right?"

"Nope. I'm an only child. I guess after my parents had me, they figured that one was enough of a pain."

"I don't believe that for a second," said Luke, smiling warmly at me.

"I've always wished I had a brother or sister," I confessed. "You're lucky to have such a big family."

Luke grinned. "Hey, how'd you like to adopt one of my brothers? Jason, for instance?"

"Oh, come on! I like Jason," I said, laughing. "But I don't really understand why you think he deliberately didn't tell you that he asked me to come over the other day."

"He figured I might tell you not to bother," Luke replied. "He probably thought he was doing me a big favor, getting a girl to visit me. Jace is quite the Don Juan in his junior high, and he's worried that his old brother is hopeless where females are concerned."

Laughing, I said, "No wonder you wanted to wring his neck!"

"Not anymore." Luke smiled at me, and I felt myself melting inside. "Actually, he *did* do me a favor."

I didn't know how to respond to that, so I said, "Well, partner, I guess we'd better get to work."

We went over to one of the couches, and after we sat down, Luke opened his guitar case

119

and took out his instrument, then pulled out several sheets of music. "I brought along some other stuff just in case you didn't like the song I told you about," he told me.

"Why don't you sing it for me?" I suggested. "I can't wait to hear it."

Luke struck a chord on the guitar. "It's called 'Chasin' after Love,' " he said, and then he started to play and sing.

All my worries quickly faded as I listened to the song. It wasn't dreadful at all. In fact, it was terrific. Until that moment, as I'd told Luke, I hadn't been a big country and western fan, but then and there I decided that I'd been more than a bit prejudiced. Luke's song told the story of two people who find true love and then lose it, so they're always chasing after the love they remember. It was funny and sweet and sad all at the same time.

"That's a wonderful song," I said when he finished. "Now I think we're a sure thing too. With that song we just can't lose!"

Luke seemed pleased. "You really like it?"

"Are you crazy? I love it! C'mon, partner, let's get to work."

I learned the song quickly, and for the next couple of hours we practiced the harmony

120

Luke had written. I was getting more and more excited. Luke's voice and mine blended perfectly, and our duet really sounded incredible.

At about four o'clock Luke put down his guitar. "Why don't we call it a day?"

"Fine by me," I said. "My throat's starting to get a little scratchy."

"And I need to stretch my legs. Would you like to take a walk?" he asked.

I nodded and we went out the back door and began walking toward the pond. It was a warm October day and the autumn foliage was at its peak. Luke stopped and gazed at the red and orange hills behind the house. "This sure is a great place you've got here."

"Yeah, it is, isn't it?" As I looked around at our land, I felt kind of like Scarlett O'Hara proudly surveying Tara.

We went down to the pond and sat on the grass, watching the ducks for quite a while. Then I suggested we go a little farther. "I want to show you my tree house," I told Luke. "Well, it's not really *my* tree house, but since I fell out of it, I guess I can make some claim to it."

Luke grinned. "Okay, but there's no way I'm climbing into the thing."

Laughing, we continued along the familiar

path that led to the woods. When we reached the tree house, we both gazed up at it. The leaves of the old tree had turned a beautiful deep shade of red. "Sure you don't want to climb up?" I asked.

"Dead sure," Luke said. "I'll just admire it from down here."

I walked over to the tree and patted its trunk. "Do you know what kind of tree this is?"

"It's a sweet gum," Luke replied matter-of-factly.

"Gee, I never even heard of that," I said. "I guess it must be native to Kentucky. . . ." I suddenly thought of Billy McConnell and looked sadly up at the tree house.

"Something wrong?" Luke asked.

"Oh, I was just thinking of Billy, the boy who built this tree house. He was Mrs. McConnell's son."

"Wasn't he killed over in Vietnam?"

I nodded. "It makes me sad thinking about how he must have loved this place and how he never came back to it. Poor Mrs. McConnell. It must have been so awful for her." I hesitated. I had never ventured to mention Luke's father before, but now I felt that I should. "I've never lost anyone I loved," I murmured. "Luke, I've heard about your father, and I just want you to know I'm really sorry."

"Thanks," he said gruffly, but I could see that he didn't want to talk about it. It was as if he had posted a Keep Out sign in front of him.

There was an awkward pause. Then Luke bent down and picked up a leaf from the ground, a beautiful dark red leaf with pointed lobes that spread out like a fan.

Taking it from him, I smiled. "Remember collecting leaves in the fall when you were a kid?"

"Sure." Luke smiled too. "I used to press them and put them in books to keep forever."

I stuck the leaf behind my ear. "What do you think? Maybe I'll start a new fashion trend."

Luke was still smiling, but as we looked at each other, his expression suddenly became serious. He leaned toward me, and I felt my heart pounding like crazy. Luke's lips were just a breath away from mine, when a loud voice shouting my name startled us both and we jumped apart.

"Tess!" came the shout again, and I frowned. It was my dad's voice. I was really irked, not to mention frustrated at being interrupted at such a romantic moment. What was he doing, anyway? Spying on us?

I sighed. "Dad? Over here," I yelled back. Looking over at Luke, I could tell that he felt the same way I did.

Soon Dad appeared from the path in the woods. "So there you are! Your mother and I were worried, Tess. We didn't know where you'd gone."

"Luke and I were just taking a walk," I said in some irritation.

"Well, it's getting late. Did you forget we're having company tonight? The Davises will be here in about an hour, and your mother could use some help."

The Davises! I'd forgotten all about them coming for dinner. I glanced at Luke but couldn't read his expression. "Okay, Dad," I said. "We'll be there in just a few minutes."

Dad looked over at Luke and said belatedly, "Of course, if you'd like to stay for dinner, Luke . . ."

"Thanks, Mr. Lawrence," he said politely, "but I've got to be getting home."

After Dad walked off down the path, I said, "I completely lost track of time. I guess we'd better start back."

"I didn't know your folks were such good

friends with the Davises," Luke said as we retraced our steps.

"Dad's gotten chummy with Judge Davis, and Mom and Mrs. Davis seem to have hit it off," I told him, "but I haven't met either of them yet. They've never been to our house before."

"Is Carter coming too?" Luke asked, his tone deliberately neutral.

"I doubt it," I said quickly. "He probably has a date."

Luke said nothing, but his expression was grim.

I sighed inwardly. What a rotten end to what had been such a promising afternoon!

We were both silent as we walked back to the house. After Luke said good-bye to my parents, I walked with him to his old pickup. He put his guitar case on the seat and turned to me. "Well, thanks for having me over, Tess. The song's coming along real well."

"It was fun," I said, smiling. "I tell you, partner, there's no doubt in my mind that we're going to win that talent show." I was glad to see an answering smile on Luke's face. "How about another practice session tomorrow?"

"Can't. I've got to work, unfortunately," he replied. "But what about after school Monday? You could come to my house this time, and maybe afterward we could go out and get something to eat."

I beamed at him. It sounded like the makings of an actual date! "That would be great," I said.

"Okay. See you Monday," Luke said, getting into the truck.

With a dreamy smile on my face I watched him drive off. Then, remembering the Davises, I hurried back to the house.

Chapter Ten

Mom said our dinner party was going to be semiformal, so after I finished giving her a hand in the kitchen, she insisted I dress up. I dutifully put on my blue dress with the scoop neck and the full skirt, hoping the evening wouldn't be too awful, and that Carter and his sister would be otherwise engaged. As I sat down at my dressing table to put on my makeup and brush my hair, I wished I were going out with Luke instead. He'd never seen me all dressed up.

Taking one last look in the mirror, I got up and went downstairs to await the Davises. I found Dad in the living room, wearing a new suit and looking as if he'd stepped right out of the pages of *GQ*. He smiled at me as I came in. "You look great, baby."

"So do you, Dad," I said. "Where's Mom?"

"She's still getting dressed. She'd better hurry too, because our guests will be arriving any minute." Just then we both heard the sound of a car on the gravel drive. "Uh-oh—that must be the Davises now," Dad said.

Mom came floating down the stairs in the nick of time. In her rose-colored silk dress and wearing a pair of dangly gold earrings, I thought she looked fabulous, like one of the jet-setting heroines in her novels.

Dad and Mom went to greet their guests at the door with me trailing reluctantly behind. Dad flung open the door just as Judge Davis and his wife were getting out of their Cadillac. The judge was tall, tanned, and athletic-looking, with graying hair that made him look very distinguished. Mrs. Davis was a very attractive, elegantly dressed blonde who looked at least ten years younger than her husband. They both smiled affably as they greeted my parents. Then the judge turned to me.

"And this lovely young lady must be Tess. No

128

wonder my boy Carter was so eager to come tonight."

My heart sank as I saw a somewhat pouty Carly and a smiling Carter get out of the car and come up the porch steps. When all the greetings and introductions were made, Mom led the way into the living room. I kept very busy helping her and Dad with drinks and hors d'oeuvres so I didn't have time to say much to Carter or his sister.

When dinner was ready, everyone took their places at our cherry-wood dining table. Mom placed Mr. and Mrs. Davis on one side of the table, and I found that I was to sit between Carter and Carly on the other.

After Mom had served the meal, Carter leaned over toward me, giving me the benefit of all his charm. "Tess, you look fabulous in that dress," he murmured.

"Thanks, Carter," I said. "You look nice too." I guess most girls would have thought "nice" a bit mild to describe Carter's appearance. He was wearing a beautifully tailored suit and with his stunning blond good looks, he could have been Robert Redford's son.

As dinner got under way, the judge, who was extremely loquacious, dominated the conversation. Finally Mrs. Davis ventured a remark on the fine fall weather we were having, and Carly said, "I sure hope it stays nice for my Halloween party next Saturday. It's such a pain when people have to come out in the rain and ruin their hair and all."

"And speaking of your party, sis . . ." Carter said, giving her a significant look.

"Oh, all right," said Carly unenthusiastically. She looked at me. "I've been meaning to ask you if you'd like to come, Tess. It's next Saturday night at eight. There'll be mostly seniors, but I always let my kid brother bring a few of his little friends along."

"That's really big of you, sis," Carter said, grinning. "Well, how about it, Tess? It's a costume party and it should be a blast."

It seemed that everyone at the table was waiting for my reply, but since I definitely didn't want to go, I found myself floundering. "It's awfully nice of you to invite me, Carly," I said, "but I don't have a costume, and—"

To my annoyance, Mom interrupted me. "Yes you do, dear. You could wear the costume you wore to Melissa's party last year." She turned to Mrs. Davis. "It was so cute. The kids all dressed up like characters in fairy tales, and Tess went as . . ." Mom glanced over at me. I guess she was taken aback by my hostile expression, because her voice trailed off.

"Let me guess," Carter said to me. "I bet you were a beautiful princess, right? Cinderella after the transformation?"

"No—Little Red Riding Hood," I mumbled.

Carter grinned. "Hey, that's cool. And since you have a costume, you've got to come."

I was trapped. Seeing no way out, I said, "Well, okay, I guess."

"Great!" said Carter.

Carly managed a tight little smile. "I'm *so* glad." Changing the subject abruptly, she added, "By the way, Tess, I heard that you're entering the talent show."

"Really, Tess?" Carter said. "What's your specialty? Baton twirling?"

"Gee, I never did master the old baton," I said sarcastically. "Actually, I'm going to sing."

"Hear that, Carly?" Carter said to his sister. "Sounds like you're going to have some competition."

Carly ignored him, focusing her attention on me. "I also heard that you're singing with Luke Stoddard."

Carter looked amazed. "You're singing with Stoddard?"

I nodded and Dad said, "As a matter of fact, the two of them were practicing at our house today. Unfortunately, Ruth and I were in town so we didn't get a chance to hear them. Tess says the Stoddard boy's quite the musician."

"And she's right," said the judge. "The kid is a chip off the old block. I remember when young Luke used to play with his daddy. Folks around here thought Charlie Stoddard would wind up at the Grand Ole Opry, but his drinking ruined him—killed him too."

"His drinking?" Mom repeated, obviously shocked.

The judge nodded sadly. "Yes, Charlie always had a fiddle or a bottle in his hands, sometimes both. I can't say anybody was surprised when he drove into that tree last year and killed himself."

"That's terrible!" Mom said as she and Dad exchanged a meaningful look. I was relieved when Mrs. Davis started talking about a new restaurant in Blossom Creek.

The rest of the evening seemed interminable. As I had anticipated, after dinner Carter, Dad, and the judge went on and on about football while the rest of us sat and listened—or, in my case, pretended to listen. I was glad when the Davises finally got ready to leave.

My parents and I walked with them to the porch, and Carter moved very close to me. "I'm real glad you're going to be my date for the party, Tess," he murmured in my ear. "I'll talk to you at school about the details, like when I'll pick you up and stuff like that."

It hadn't occurred to me until that very moment that I'd be going to Carly's party as Carter's date. Now that he had pointed it out to me, I wasn't happy, not one bit.

As soon as Carter and his family drove off in their big Caddy, Mom, Dad, and I went back into the house and flopped into chairs in the living room. "Let's clean up tomorrow, honey," Dad said. "I'm bushed."

"You won't get any argument from me on that," said Mom. She smiled at me. "Carter certainly seems like a nice boy—so polite, and so well dressed."

"And he sure knows his football," Dad added.

I shrugged irritably. "I don't like football, or football players."

"I know. You like the more artistic types,

right, kiddo?" Dad teased. "Like musicians, for example."

"Give me a break, Dad," I groaned.

"Tess," Mom said hesitantly, "did you know about Luke's father?" I nodded. "Why didn't you tell us about him?"

I shrugged. "I don't know. I guess it just never came up." Seeing Mom's worried expression, I sighed. "So what's the big deal?"

"Well, dear, it sounds as if Luke comes from a . . . well, a bad family situation," she said.

"Yeah—it's pretty bad having your father killed in a car accident," I snapped.

"But apparently his father was an alcoholic."

"That's not Luke's fault, is it?" I asked belligerently.

"Of course not," said Mom. "It's just that . . ." She looked over at Dad for assistance.

"Don't get mad, Tess," he said. "Your mother and I are just concerned about you, that's all."

"Well, you don't have to be," I told him. "I'm not a baby, you know." Standing up, I added, "And now, if you'll excuse me, I think I'll go to bed."

As I got undressed and put on my pajamas, I thought about the day's events. I had almost been kissed by Luke, which was wonderful, but it seemed that I was going to a stupid Halloween party with Carter, which wasn't wonderful at all. Even less wonderful was the fact that my parents obviously preferred Carter to Luke.

Oh, why can't things just be simple? I thought sadly as I crawled into bed.

On Monday morning, as I was walking into the chemistry classroom, I was stopped right inside the door by Carter's voice behind me calling my name. I turned around and he smiled. "Hi, Tess. Listen, I sure had a terrific time at your house Saturday."

At that moment Luke came through the door. He gave us both a brief glance and would have kept going if Carter hadn't spoken to him. "Hey, Stoddard," he said, "I hear you're singing a duet with Tess in the talent show. That's great." He slapped Luke on the back, which Luke didn't seem to appreciate, and then turned back to me. "I can't wait to hear you sing, Tess. And I can't wait to see your costume, either."

"Costume?" Luke repeated. "What costume?"

Carter grinned. "Oh, not for your act, Stoddard, although it might be a good idea. I meant Tess's costume for the Halloween party I'm taking her to on Saturday night. She's going as Little Red Riding Hood." He leaned toward me, leering. "You better watch out for the Big Bad Wolf, Little Red."

Glancing helplessly at Luke, I saw that the old familiar Stoddard scowl had reappeared. He didn't say anything, just walked back to our lab table.

"It looks like Stoddard got out on the wrong side of the bed this morning," Carter joked. "You better try and cheer him up, Tess. I've got to talk to Brad about something for a minute. See you later." With that, he went out into the hall.

I quickly joined Luke at our lab table. He had taken out his chemistry homework and was scowling down at it.

"Luke?" I said hesitantly. He looked up, still scowling. "Listen, about me going out with Carter—" I began.

Luke cut me off. "Hey, it's none of my business who you go out with."

"You see," I continued, deciding to ignore his hostile attitude, "he came to dinner at my house Saturday night with his folks—"

136

"I thought you said he had a date," Luke broke in again.

"I just said I thought he *might* have a date," I said, frowning. "Will you please stop interrupting and listen to me? Anyway, he didn't, and neither did Carly, so they came, and Carly mentioned this party she's having Saturday night, and then Carter kind of made her invite me, and I couldn't very well refuse."

"Why not?"

"Well, it was sort of awkward. I mean, their parents were there and everything . . ."

Luke looked back down at his homework. "Oh, well, that explains it, then," he said sarcastically.

I regarded him in frustration. "C'mon, Luke! I don't really want to go to this party, with or without Carter. Maybe I can get out of it."

"Why should you, Little Red? I'm sure you'll have a terrific time with the Big Bad Wolf."

"Give me a break, Luke." I sighed. "I just told you I didn't want to go. Please let's not fight. We're partners, remember, and we have a rehearsal at your house after school today."

"Let's just forget the whole thing, okay?" he muttered.

"Forget what?"

"The rehearsal. The act. The talent show. Forget it."

I stared at him. "You don't want to perform in the show anymore? Or do you mean you just don't want to perform with me?" He didn't answer, and I angrily sat down next to him. "Fine, if that's the way you want it!" I opened up my chemistry notebook and tried very hard not to burst into tears.

Chapter Eleven

On Saturday night I sat in my room, braiding my hair, and reflecting on what a rotten week it had been. Luke hadn't spoken to me since our conversation Monday morning, and since I was totally crazy about the guy, I was totally miserable.

Carter, on the other hand, was obviously trying to heat things up. He'd spread the word that he was taking me to Carly's Halloween party, and we were already becoming an item on the B.C. romance grapevine. My girlfriends, especially Dawn Ritter, were all envious of my huge coup in getting a date with Carter. Well, not *all* my girlfriends. Lenny made it clear that she was disappointed in me, which made things even worse since her opinion was the only one that really mattered.

I sighed as I finished my last braid. I sure wasn't looking forward to Carly's party. For one thing, there would be a bunch of seniors there that I didn't even know, and for another, the idea of going with Carter wasn't thrilling me at all.

What's your problem? I asked my pigtailed reflection in the mirror. *Luke made it very clear that he doesn't want to have anything more to do with you. And any girl at school—except Lenny, of course—would give their right arm to go to this party with Carter Davis. After all, Carter's popular, handsome, and rich. What more could a girl possibly ask for?*

I frowned, studying myself in the mirror. There was still another reason I was dreading the party. I felt ridiculous in my Little Red Riding Hood costume. It had been fun at Melissa's party last year when the other kids were dressed as Cinderella, or Rumpelstiltskin, or Goldilocks and the Three Bears, but I knew that Carly and her friends would think it was unsophisticated and definitely uncool. I felt like a little kid again, when I would decide at the last minute that I didn't like my Halloween costume and drive Mom crazy with my fussing until she came up with something else for me to wear.

Getting up from my dressing table, I went over to the bed and grabbed my hooded red cloak. After I put it on, I looked into the mirror again and cringed. Yes, I definitely looked ridiculous, I thought dismally. I was wearing a short Austrian-type dirndl under the red cloak, and my hair hung down in two braids from underneath the roomy hood. I suddenly wished I were on my way to Granny's house instead of Carly's party.

Heaving another sigh, I picked up the basket that I would use for a purse and went downstairs. Mom and Dad beamed at me as I walked into the living room.

"You look absolutely adorable, honey," Mom said.

"You sure do, kiddo," said Dad. "But don't forget to watch out for the—"

"Big Bad Wolf. I know, Dad," I said with a groan, realizing that I'd probably be hearing that line for the rest of the evening. I sat down on the couch to wait for Carter. I didn't have to wait very long before I heard a car pull up in front of the house.

"That must be Carter. I'll get it," I said as I walked out of the room to the foyer. But when I opened the front door, there was no one there. "Carter?" I called, peering around.

Then a voice came from behind the porch swing. "Little Red Riding Hood," it said. I could tell right away it was Carter doing a bad impression of somebody, probably some actor I'd never heard of. "When you go out into the woods tonight, watch out for—"

I rolled my eyes. "I know," I interrupted. "The Big Bad Wolf!"

"No, Little Red, the Big—Bad—" Suddenly Carter leapt out from behind the swing. "Psychopath!" he shouted. I jumped about a foot, and he laughed maniacally. Carter was wearing a Freddy Krueger mask and wielding a bloody fake knife—or at least I hoped it was fake.

"Very funny, Carter," I said dryly.

He took off the mask and grinned. "Hey, I couldn't find a wolf costume." Coming over to me, Carter purred, "You look great, Red—good enough to eat."

"Thanks, I think," I muttered. "Come on in,

Freddy, and say hello to my parents. But don't murder them or anything, okay?"

Carter laughed, and after we went in for the usual parental greeting, we left for Carter's house. On the way there, we picked up Brad Robinson and his date, Mandy Palmer. Although I didn't know Brad very well and I'd never even met Mandy, I was relieved to discover that we would be on a double date. Brad was dressed as one of the characters on *Star Trek*. Mandy, a cute little brunette who giggled at everything Brad said as if he were one of the greatest comedians on earth, was dressed as a punk rock star. No question about it, I was totally out of place as Little Red Riding Hood.

The Davises lived in a large Victorian mansion in the section of town where all the wealthy doctors and lawyers resided. It really was a great house, with turrets and towers and lots of gingerbread decoration. There was a circular drive in front of the house, and it was easy to imagine the old days, when people would have driven up to parties there in carriages. Tonight there were no carriages in the drive, but there were plenty of cars parked around it. It looked as if Carly was having quite a crowd. As Carter opened the car door for me,

I began to think the evening might not be quite so awful as I'd feared.

There were a number of candlelit jack-o'-lanterns and a Frankenstein dummy sitting on the porch. Brad patted the dummy on the head as we passed it, saying, "Hey, dude, lookin' good!" Mandy giggled and gave me a look that meant "Is this guy a riot, or what?"

Just then the door opened and we were greeted by Carly. She looked utterly fabulous in a *Gone With the Wind* gown with her blond hair piled high on top of her head. She stepped out onto the porch, languidly waving a huge fan.

"And what have we here?" she asked, looking at Brad and raising her eyebrows. "Not another Trekkie!"

"You mean the rest of the *Enterprise* crew is here?" Brad said. Mandy giggled, of course.

"Carly, you look sensational," I said politely.

She favored me with a little queenly smile. "Thanks, Tess. And your costume is just *too* cute." Somehow the way she said it didn't sound like a compliment, but I managed to smile back at her.

"Well, c'mon, gang," said Carter, "let's party!" We all trooped inside the house,

where a mob of kids was milling around, talking and laughing. Monsters and rock stars
seemed to be the costumes of choice. Carter
took my hand. "There's dancing up in the
ballroom."

"The ballroom?" I echoed. "You have a
ballroom?"

Carter shrugged. "Doesn't everybody?" He
pulled me after him through the crowded hall
and up a winding staircase. At the top was a
huge room filled with costumed kids dancing
to the loud music that blasted from speakers
placed at either end. As we joined the rest of
the dancing crowd, I began to think the evening might actually turn out to be fun.

After we had been dancing for some time,
Carter suggested, "How about something to
drink?"

That sounded good to me. I was pretty
thirsty. We went back downstairs, and I followed Carter to the dining room, where every
conceivable kind of munchies and junk food
was being devoured. I pitied whoever would
have to clean up after the party. We didn't stop
there, though. Carter led me into a huge
kitchen, where a lot of ice-filled buckets were
lined up on the table. Most of the buckets con-

tained sodas, but several had cans of beer in them.

"Your folks let you have beer at your parties?" I asked in surprise.

Carter grinned. "My old man may be a judge, but he's okay. From what I understand, he hoisted quite a few back in his young days. He and Mom are great about things like this. When Carly and I have parties, they just clear out and give us our space."

"Your parents aren't here?" I asked. I guess I sounded a little shocked, because Carter laughed.

"Heck, no. The only thing they ask is that we don't totally trash the place." Carter took two beers out of the bucket and handed one to me. I hate the taste of beer, and I didn't really want it, but I also didn't want Carter to think I was uncool or anything, so I went ahead and took a sip. Carter took some long chugs on his can and was soon getting another one. "Hey, drink up, Red," he said. "You're way behind me."

"No thanks," I said. "I'm fine, really." As I watched Carter gulp down his second beer, I was getting a little uncomfortable. "How about something to eat?" I suggested brightly.

He came closer and put an arm around me.

"You hungry, little girl?" I laughed and pulled away. His breath smelled like beer, and I was beginning to feel really nervous. Then Brad and Mandy and a couple of other kids burst into the kitchen. They started drinking beer and horsing around. The guys began playing basketball with the empty beer cans, shooting them at the sink and cheering loudly when they clattered inside.

I was glad when Carly came into the kitchen and eyed the guys disgustedly. "Cut it out, you morons," she said. "You're going to scratch up the sink."

"Take it easy, sis. You're ruining all our fun," said Carter. He gulped the last of his beer and threw the can at the sink. It missed by a mile, clanging against the stove.

"I said cut it out, Carter!" Carly snapped.

Carter just walked over and got himself another beer, his fifth by my count. He smiled at Carly and then tossed the full can at the sink.

"Carter!" Carly yelled. "This is my party, and I don't want you fouling it up!"

Carter pulled on his Freddy Krueger mask and growled, "Is that any way to talk to a psychopath?"

"You're a real comedian," she said, eyeing him with a contemptuous expression.

"Okay, okay. We'll leave you to your stupid party," Carter said. "C'mon, Brad, Mandy—we're gonna go howl at the moon." He suddenly seemed to remember my existence and grabbed my arm. "You come too, Red."

The four of us went out the back door and to my dismay, Carter and Brad actually stood in the yard and began howling. Looking at the houses next door, I wondered what the people inside were thinking. Just another of the Davis kids' crazy parties?

"Let's go for a drive," Carter said suddenly. Putting his arm around my shoulders, he added, "Or better yet, let's go park."

"Right!" Brad shouted. He and Mandy ran around the house toward the front.

"Uh—Carter," I said hesitantly. "I don't know if you should drive. I mean, you've been drinking . . ."

He looked annoyed. "I just had a few beers. No big deal. But if you insist . . ."

Carter all but dragged me to the circular driveway, where Brad and Mandy were waiting next to his car. Carter tossed his car keys to

Brad. "Here, buddy—you get to drive. Tess and I will take the backseat."

I wasn't too pleased with this setup, either, since it seemed to me that Brad had been drinking just as much as Carter. As soon as we climbed into the backseat, Carter pulled me toward him and started covering my face with sloppy kisses. I struggled, and managed to fight him off.

He scowled at me. "What's your problem, Red?"

I didn't say anything. Brad looked back at us. "Something wrong?" he asked.

"No," Carter muttered. "Hit the road, pal. Let's cruise the main drag."

As Brad drove and honked along the street, Carter moved in on me again, but I squirmed away and peered through the car window.

"What's so fascinating out there?" He leaned across me and looked out too. "Isn't that Stoddard's pickup truck at the Winn Dixie?"

My heart skipped a beat. Turning my head, I looked back at the market we had just passed. Sure enough, there was Luke's truck parked in front. "Is that what you were so interested in?" he asked.

"I didn't even see it until now," I protested.

Carter snorted. "Right! Hey, Captain Kirk," he yelled to Brad. "Go around the block and pull up in front of the Winn Dixie, will you? I have a sudden craving for a Twinkie."

"Carter . . ." I warned.

"I just want a Twinkie, okay?" he said innocently. "Nothing the matter with that, is there?"

Brad drove around the block, and as he neared the Winn Dixie store, Carter ordered, "Pull up next to Stoddard's rust bucket."

Brad obediently parked next to Luke's truck and then turned around with a questioning look on his face. Carter pulled out a bill from his wallet and handed it to him. "Go buy some stuff, will you? And Mandy, why don't you go with him? He may need some help." As Brad and Mandy got out of the car, Carter added, "Take your time!"

Then he turned to me and grinned. "We needed some privacy, Little Red."

"I don't call this very private," I said irritably, glad that Luke was nowhere in sight.

Carter slid very close to me and put both arms around me. "It's plenty private enough for me," he said, pulling me toward him and planting a long, beery kiss on my lips. When I shoved him away, he cursed. "What's with you tonight, Tess?"

"I just don't feel like it," I snapped.

"Yeah, right. I bet you'd feel like it if Stoddard were here with you."

"Don't be such a creep, Carter!" I moved as far away from him as I could get.

Neither of us said another word until Brad and Mandy came back to the car. Brad threw a bag into Carter's lap. "Your Twinkies, sir," he said. "I got some more beers, too."

Carter dropped the bag on the floor and opened his door. "I'm going to drive now. You and Mandy get in back," he commanded, getting out of the car. "Tess, come up front with me."

As Brad and Mandy climbed in the backseat, I got out and walked over to the driver's side. "Listen, Carter," I said, "I really don't want to ride with you. I'm going to call my parents to come and get me."

Carter stared at me. "You're *what*? You've got to be kidding! Call your parents? No way!" I started to back away, but he grabbed my arm. "Get in. You're coming with me."

I was struggling to get out of his grasp, when

a deep voice behind me said, "What's going on?" I looked over my shoulder and saw Luke and his brother Jason with grocery sacks in their arms.

"Nothing, Stoddard," Carter muttered. "Mind your own business!"

"Is there a problem, Tess?" Luke asked quietly.

"I just—I just want to go home, that's all," I stammered.

"I'll take you home," Carter growled. "Now, will you just get in the car?"

"No!" I exclaimed. "I'm not riding with you. You've had too much to drink, Carter. You shouldn't be driving at all."

Luke walked over to the pickup and dropped his bags into the back. Then he turned around. "I'll drive you home, Tess."

"Oh, yeah? Over my dead body!" Carter said.

Jason looked up expectantly at his big brother.

"Tess is right, Davis," Luke said evenly. "If you've been drinking, you shouldn't be driving."

"Thanks for the lecture, Stoddard," Carter sneered. "But you should have given it to your old man instead of me."

152

Luke clenched his fists. I thought he might take a swing at Carter, but he managed to control himself.

"You son of a—" Jason began, moving menacingly toward Carter.

"Jace!" Luke said. "Put the bags in the truck."

"But Luke . . ."

His brother gave him a look, and Jason stomped over to the truck.

Then Luke looked at me. "Get in the truck, Tess," he said calmly.

I hurried away from Carter and climbed into Luke's pickup. Carter started to come after me, but Luke grabbed him. "Forget it, Davis!"

As I watched in horror, Carter shoved Luke and then threw a punch at him. Luke dodged and Carter stumbled, almost losing his balance. Jason ran over, eager to get into the fracas, but Luke grabbed him. "Get in the truck, Jace," he ordered. *"Now!"*

Jason seemed about to protest, but then got into the truck next to me. Carter was leaning against his car, looking a little groggy. Luke didn't say anything to him. He just walked over to the pickup and got into the driver's seat. As he put the truck in reverse and backed out of the parking space, Carter shouted, "You're scum, Stoddard, you and your whole family!"

I glanced nervously at Luke, but he didn't react at all. As we drove off, Carter was pounding his fist on the hood of his car, and I sighed in relief at my lucky escape. However, when I glanced at Luke again and saw his grim expression, I wondered if "lucky" was the right word.

Chapter Twelve

There was a tense, awkward silence as we rode along. I was wedged in between Luke and Jason, and all three of us were staring glumly out the front windshield. At last Jason spoke. "You should have punched him out, Luke."

I looked at Luke and could see him frowning. "Oh, yeah? What good would that have done?"

"The creep was asking for it, making that crack about Daddy the way he did," Jason said angrily, ignoring Luke's question. When Luke didn't respond, Jason continued. "I would've put my fist right in his stupid face. . . ."

155

"I know. That's why I told you to get in the truck," said his brother dryly.

Jason made an exasperated sound and looked out the side window. Then he turned back to his brother. "Daddy always said we shouldn't run away from a fight."

Luke sighed. "I wasn't running away from a fight, Jace. I was avoiding one."

"What's the difference?" Jason asked. "Daddy always said . . ."

"Well now, Daddy wasn't always right, was he?" Luke said bitterly. I expected Jason to fly into a rage at this comment, but he just stared out the window again.

I fidgeted uncomfortably between the two brothers. I was grateful to them for rescuing me, but I got the strong impression that neither of them thought very highly of me for getting into a situation where I needed rescuing. Sneaking another glance at Luke, I saw that he was still frowning. No doubt he would be glad to get rid of me.

I hadn't been paying attention to where we were going, so when Luke turned onto Peach Street and then pulled up in front of his house, I was surprised. So was Jason.

"I thought we were driving Tess home."

"No, *we're* not driving her home. We're dropping off these groceries at the house and then *you're* putting them away while *I* drive her home."

I looked over at Jason and met his gaze. He suddenly smiled at me. "See what a bossy brother I've got, Tess?" His smile broadened. "Hey, I never said how cute you look in that costume. Doesn't she look cute, Luke?" he asked. Luke didn't say a word. Jason went on. "I was wondering, Tess—would you consider going out with an eighth-grader? A *mature* eighth-grader?"

I couldn't help grinning.

"Oh, shut up, Jace," Luke muttered.

Jason just laughed. "Hey, you can't blame a guy for trying," he said. "Well, Tess, I guess I'd better get a move on, or my big brother will be on my case again." Lowering his voice, he added, "You know, Luke can be a pain sometimes, but he's really not such a bad guy."

"Jason!" Luke shouted. "The groceries!"

He and Jason got out, took the grocery sacks out of the back of the truck, and then carried them inside. Luke reappeared a couple of minutes later and climbed back into the truck. Without speaking he turned the key in the ignition and we were on our way again.

We rode in silence for a while. When Luke turned the pickup onto the highway that led out of town, I couldn't stand it anymore. "Luke . . ." I began somewhat hesitantly. "I—well, I just want to thank you for coming to my rescue like that."

Luke only grunted.

I sighed in exasperation. "You know, Jason was right about you, Luke Stoddard!" Luke glanced at me with a quizzical expression. "Sometimes you can be a real pain!" Then I smiled at him. "But you're really not such a bad guy."

I saw a slight answering smile appear on his face. "Careful, Tess. A compliment like that might go to my head."

"That's better." I took a deep breath. "Luke, can we be friends again?"

There was another long silence. Finally he said, "I guess so, if that's what you want."

"What do *you* want?" I asked in frustration.

Instead of answering, Luke glanced in his rearview mirror. "This jerk is really riding my bumper!" he muttered.

I turned my head around and saw a car's bright headlights a few feet behind us. "I hate it when people do that," I said. "Why doesn't the idiot just go ahead and pass if he's in such a hurry?"

As I spoke, the car swerved into the other lane and speeded up. "Good riddance!" I said. Then the car pulled next to us and started honking.

Luke frowned. "What the—"

I looked over and was horrified to realize that the car was Carter's. It shot past, and soon its taillights were way ahead of us. I sighed in relief. Carter was in such a state that I had been afraid he would do something stupid, like challenge Luke to a race or something.

"He shouldn't be driving," Luke said angrily.

"I know." I hesitated. "Listen, Luke, I was telling you the truth when I said I didn't want to go to that party with Carter. I was having a rotten time too."

Luke suddenly grinned at me. "Good! I'm glad you had a rotten time." I burst out laughing. "Tess . . . " he began more seriously, then broke off at the sight of a car speeding toward us in the other lane. I couldn't be sure, but I thought it was Carter's again.

"He must have turned around," I said nervously. As the car got closer to Luke's pickup, it suddenly lurched into our lane. I screamed and Luke spun the wheel sharply to the right. As the truck went skidding off onto the shoulder, I grabbed the seat in terror and closed my eyes tight, thinking it was all over. Somehow, Luke managed to keep control of the vehicle and we came to an abrupt halt, narrowly missing a fence.

I was so shaken that I just sat there for a second, too stunned to move. As my fear receded, it was replaced by anger. Looking out the back window, I saw that Carter's car had stopped on the other side of the highway. I wrenched open my door, jumped out of the truck, and screamed, "You moron! You could have killed us!"

I was about to go over and give Carter a real piece of my mind, when the car started up again. It pulled back onto the highway and gunned away. "Idiots!" I shouted after it, waving my fist. Then I marched back to the pickup and got inside. "Can you *believe* that guy?" I exclaimed.

I suddenly noticed that Luke was sitting stone still with his head bowed and his hands clenched on the steering wheel, and my panic returned. "Luke!" I cried. "What's wrong?"

He slowly raised his head, and when he turned to look at me, I had never seen such a look of misery on a human face. "Why did he have to do it? *Why?*" he moaned.

It took me a moment to realize that Luke wasn't talking about Carter Davis. He was talking about Charlie Stoddard.

I put my hand on his arm. "Luke . . ." I said gently. "Oh, Luke . . ."

He blinked and seemed to come out of it. "I'm sorry, Tess," he said gruffly. "I guess I was a little shook up. I'm okay now."

I figured Luke was going to clam up again and somehow I didn't think that was a good thing, so I plunged ahead. "You were thinking about your father, weren't you? About his accident?"

A struggle seemed to be going on within Luke. Suddenly he began pounding his fist against the steering wheel. "It was so stupid, getting tanked up and driving into a tree like that! Of all the stupid, selfish things to do!" He turned to me. "Daddy always used to say, 'When your number's up, your number's up,' like you had no choice at all in the matter.

Well, he *did* have a choice and he made it and he got himself killed." He shook his head and continued bitterly. "His family wasn't enough for him. The music wasn't enough for him. He just had to have the booze . . ." Luke's voice choked up.

I moved closer and put my arm around him. "I'm so sorry, Luke," I whispered around the lump in my own throat.

When he could speak again, he said, "I loved him, Tess, but he made me so mad. Even though he's dead, he still makes me mad!"

Luke suddenly began telling me about his father. At first he talked angrily about his father's drinking, but then he started remembering the good times when he was growing up. He even smiled as he related a few stories about his childhood. "Ma always said Daddy was teaching me to play the fiddle even before I could walk," he said.

That made me smile too. "I can just imagine you as a baby with a bib and a fiddle under your chin."

He laughed. "That's about the size of it." Then, embarrassed, he looked away from me, out at the darkened field. "Sorry, Tess," he mumbled. "I've been talking your ear off."

"I don't mind. It's about time you let it all out," I said softly.

"Well, it's getting late. I better get you home, or your folks will start worrying." Luke started the truck and carefully drove off the shoulder onto the highway.

A few minutes later he pulled up in front of my house. Luke turned to me and said, "Thanks a lot, Tess."

"What do you mean? You rescued me, remember?"

He shook his head. "You know. For listening."

I smiled at him. "What are friends for? And by the way, partner," I continued, "let's sing in the talent show, okay? I mean, we make a terrific team. Such talent shouldn't be wasted, right?"

"Right—partner." And then he leaned over and kissed me.

I threw my arms around his neck and kissed him back. About a dozen kisses later, Luke grinned at me. "I kind of like this teamwork stuff."

Laughing, I said, "So do I! But I'd better go in now before my parents get out the binoculars to see what's happening out here."

163

"Do you want me to come in with you?" Luke asked.

I shook my head. "No, that's okay. I want to tell them the whole story myself—about how Prince Charming came by on his white charger and rescued Little Red Riding Hood."

"Hold it, Miss Hood," said Luke with a grin. "I think you've got your fairy tales mixed up. There's no Prince Charming in Little Red Riding Hood. Isn't it a lumberjack or something?"

"Okay, so I've got the wrong fairy tale," I said. I quickly kissed him again. "But I *do* have the right prince!"

Naturally, my parents were horrified by my tale of the Halloween party and Carter's behavior. When I told them how Luke had handled the situation, they were cautiously impressed; I could tell they still had their doubts about him. That didn't bother me, though. I figured they would wise up sooner or later. Parents can be a little slow about some things, you know.

Sure enough, it didn't take long for Mom and Dad to discover what a good guy Luke was. When he came to our house to practice for the talent show, he was unfailingly polite, and once he started loosening up a bit and cracked a joke or two, they really began to like him.

During the three weeks before the show, I was also spending a lot of time at Luke's house. It was a little strange at first, always having such a mob of people around, but after a while I started feeling right at home. Luke's brothers, Jim, Davey, Sam, and Jason, all became individuals rather than just a bunch of noisy boys. Of course, Jason had always been an individual to me. He could still be a world class smart aleck sometimes, but I was becoming fond of him.

Although I had been pretty nervous about meeting Luke's mother, I felt a lot better when I found out that she was just as nervous about meeting me. Mrs. Stoddard was a dark-haired, quiet woman who reminded me a lot of Luke. She often had the same solemn, worried expression that Luke used to have, and I found myself wishing that she would smile more.

Annie and I continued to hit it off. On her sixth birthday in November, I got her a little stuffed black and white horse. "Oh, it's so cute!" she cried, and gave me a hug. "I'll call it Tess." That really got me. I mean, it's not every day that you have a stuffed animal named after you.

As for Carter Davis, on the Monday after the Halloween party he actually apologized to Luke and me. He admitted to behaving like a jerk and agreed that he had been drinking too much. Luke accepted his apology more graciously than I did—I was still furious that he'd almost gotten us all killed. But after a while I was at least able to be civil to him. Not that Carter seemed to care. He quickly started dating a friend of Mandy Palmer's, who seemed to worship him no matter what moronic thing he did.

In no time at all it was the night of the talent show. I was so nervous I could hardly stand it. As Luke and I waited backstage at the high school auditorium with the rest of the performers, I began tapping my foot so fast that Luke grinned at me and said, "I hope you're going to slow down the tempo a bit when we start singing."

"Sorry," I mumbled. "I've just got a bad case of the jitters." I eyed Carly Davis enviously. She looked beautiful, as usual, and totally calm and self-possessed. "Look at Carly," I said to Luke. "She doesn't look one bit jittery!"

166

"Appearances can be deceiving," Luke said. "I bet inside she's scared to death." Then he grinned. "I know I am. I hope I don't have a heart attack when it's our turn."

Lenny suddenly came hurrying over to us. "Hey, you guys, I just wanted to wish you good luck. I know you'll be great."

"Thanks, Lenny," I said. "I'll just be happy if I don't foul up."

"You won't," she stated confidently. "You and Luke are terrific together. You're going to blow Carly away. Well, I guess I'd better go find my seat. Break a leg, you hear?"

Luke groaned. "Don't say that, Lenny! Tess might take it literally."

After Lenny left, Luke and I waited while one act after another took the stage. It seemed like an eternity until it was finally our turn to sing. We stood in the wings while Mr. Cassin introduced us.

"And now," he announced, "Luke Stoddard and Tess Lawrence are going to sing a song that Luke wrote called 'Chasin' after Love'."

As we walked onto the stage, my knees felt more than a little wobbly, but when I looked over at Luke, his warm, loving smile gave me courage. The minute we began to sing, I lost my stage fright. In fact, I even started enjoying myself. When we finished and the audience burst into loud applause and cheers, I knew we were a hit.

There were still some kids performing after us, including Carly, so Luke and I went backstage again to wait. I knew how much winning that scholarship money meant to Luke, and as we waited, I crossed all my fingers for luck.

Finally, the last performer came off the stage. It was time for the judges to make their decision. After a short time, a couple of kids ran in all excited. "Carly!" one of them squealed. "Get out there!"

My heart sank. So Carly Davis had won after all. I looked sadly at Luke. "I thought for sure we'd win."

"What do you mean? We haven't lost yet."

"But Carly . . ."

"There are three prizes being given out, remember?" he said. "Carly must have won third."

Just then another kid rushed in to call Bobby Marshall, the school's star trumpet player, to the stage. The suspense was killing me. I grabbed Luke's hand and hung on tight.

Suddenly I heard somebody shout, "Luke and Tess!" The other contestants cheered as we made our way to the stage, grinning from ear to ear. Mr. Cassin was out there and so was Blossom Creek's most famous son, Tommy Lee Redmond. Tommy Lee turned out to be a tall, bearded man in a white suit with sequins on the lapels. He beamed at Luke and me as we approached.

"Congratulations!" Mr. Cassin said.

"Hey, you kids," said Tommy Lee, enthusiastically shaking first my hand and then Luke's, "that's one great act you got there. Great song, too."

The crowd cheered, whistled, and clapped. I was so excited that I impulsively hugged both Mr. Cassin and Tommy Lee Redmond.

"Hey, what about me?" Luke asked, pretending to be hurt. I laughed and then hugged him too.

As Mr. Cassin handed over the check, I wished there were some way I could persuade Luke to take the whole thing. He really needed the money, and I didn't.

Tommy Lee shook our hands again and then he clapped Luke on the back. "I was always a big fan of your daddy's," he said.

"Thanks," said Luke. "He was a big fan of yours too."

Tommy Lee went on. "Listen, Luke, like I said, that's a great song you wrote. I'm hoping you'll let me record it."

Luke's jaw dropped. He looked temporarily stunned, but finally managed to stammer, "You—you want to record 'Chasin' after Love'?"

"I sure do, buddy. And if it's the hit I think it will be, this here scholarship money will seem like a drop in the bucket."

Luke was too shocked to speak, so I spoke for him. "That's wonderful, Mr. Redmond," I cried.

He smiled at me. "Call me Tommy Lee, darlin'."

After the show Lenny and my other friends rushed up to congratulate Luke and me, followed by my parents and the whole Stoddard clan. Then Dr. Barry wedged his way through the crowd. "You were terrific, Tess," he said, smiling.

"You certainly were," said the woman behind him. As she moved forward to take my hand, I saw that it was Mrs. McConnell. She was all dressed up, and she looked great. "Mrs. McConnell!" I exclaimed. "I'm so glad to see you! I didn't know you were coming."

"Well, Jeff dropped by to see me one day and

he mentioned about you being in the talent show. He suggested I go with him and his family."

As if on cue, a short blond woman appeared next to Mrs. McConnell with two little red-haired boys in tow.

"This is my wife, Susie," said Dr. Barry. "And these are my sons, Mike and Billy."

Mrs. McConnell smiled at me a little wistfully. "They remind me of their father and *my* Billy when they were that age," she said.

"Mom," said the older of the boys, "Mrs. Mac said we could come out to her place in the country. She says there's an old tree house there we could play in if Dad fixes it up a bit. Isn't that cool?"

"Definitely cool," said Mrs. Barry.

Before they left, Mrs. McConnell whispered to me, "That Luke Stoddard seems like a real nice boy, Tess. I'd hang on to him if I was you."

I grinned. "I intend to!"

She grinned back and then, taking Dr. Barry's arm, she walked off through the crowd with Mrs. Barry and the two boys following behind.

Mrs. Stoddard surprised me by shyly inviting my parents and me to come over to her house for some pecan pie. Mom and Dad promptly accepted, and I went backstage with Luke so he could get his guitar.

"Well, partner," I said, "we did it!"

He smiled. "Yeah, partner, we sure did."

"I can't get over Tommy Lee wanting to record 'Chasin' after Love,' " I said happily. "I just know it will be a big hit. Then you can start recording your own songs. Gee, you'll probably become rich and famous!" I paused, picturing Luke as a country and western star. "Pretty soon you'll be wearing one of those sequined suits like Tommy Lee's, and I bet you'll have a whole bunch of C & W groupies who look like Dolly Parton hanging around, madly in love with you."

"That sounds real fine to me," Luke said with a mischievous grin.

I playfully punched his shoulder. "Luke Stoddard! You cut that out!"

Still grinning, he pulled me into his arms. "Just kidding, Tess. You know I don't want any of that." He kissed me lightly on the nose. "I have all the love I need right here." And then he kissed me very sweetly on the lips.